CLIVILIUS
WHERE CREATION MEETS INFINITY

© 2024 Nathan Cowdrey. All rights reserved.
First Edition, 12 March 2024
ISBN 978-1-4461-1484-1
Imprint: Lulu.com

Step into Clivilius, where creation meets infinity, and the essence of reality is yours to redefine. Here, existence weaves into a narrative where every decision has consequences, every action has an impact, and every moment counts. In this realm, shaped by the visionary AI CLIVE, inhabitants are not mere spectators but pivotal characters in an evolving drama where the lines between worlds blur.

Guardians traverse the realms of Clivilius and Earth, their journeys igniting events that challenge the balance between these interconnected universes. The quest for resources and the enigma of unexplained disappearances on Earth mirror the deeper conflicts and intricacies that define Clivilius—a world where reality responds to the collective will and individual choices of its Clivilians, revealing a complex interplay of creation, control, and consequence.

In the grand tapestry of Clivilius, the struggle for harmony and the dance of dichotomies play out across a cosmic stage. Here, every soul's journey contributes to the narrative, where the lines between utopia and dystopia, creator and observer, become increasingly fluid. Clivilius is not just a realm to be explored but a reality to be shaped.

Open your eyes. Expand your mind. Experience your new reality. Welcome to Clivilius, where the journey of discovery is not just about seeing a new world but about seeing your world anew.

Also in the Clivilius Series:

Sarah Lahey (4338.209.1 - 4338.214.2)

In the grip of Tasmania's eerie disappearances, Detective Sarah Lahey's quest for answers becomes a personal crucible. As her investigation draws her deeper into the shadows, her tangled relationship with fellow detective Karl Jenkins blurs the lines between ally and liability. Together, they face a darkening path that tests their bond and the very heart of their resolve. "Sarah Lahey" weaves a tale of relentless pursuit and suspense, where the quest for truth risks more than just a partnership—it tempts a treacherous fate.

Gladys Cramer (4338.205.1 - 4338.214.3)

In a world frayed by tragedies, Gladys Cramer seeks solace in wine, her steadfast refuge amid life's turmoil. Tethered to a man ensnared by duty and love, she stands at a pivotal crossroads, her choices poised to weave the threads of her fate. Each glass of wine deepens her reflection on the decisions looming ahead and the silent vows brimming with untold consequences. Amidst tragedy and secrets, with wine as her guiding light yet potential harbinger of misstep, Gladys's journey veers onto a path set for an inevitable collision.

Beatrix Cramer (4338.205.1 - 4338.211.6)

Beatrix Cramer's life is a delicate balance of contradictions, her independence and keen intellect shadowed by her penchant for the forbidden. A master of acquisition, her love for antiques and the call of the wild drives her into the heart of danger, making her an indispensable ally yet an unpredictable force. When fate thrusts her into the clandestine world of Guardians, Beatrix must navigate a labyrinth of secrets and moral dilemmas. Caught in the crossfire of legacy and destiny, she faces choices that could redefine the boundaries of her world and her very identity.

Jamie Greyson (4338.204.1 - 4338.209.3)

Haunted by shadows of his past, Jamie Greyson navigates life with a guarded heart, his complex bond with Luke Smith teetering on the brink of collapse. When Jamie is thrust into a strange new world, every moment is a test, pushing him to confront not only the dangers that lurk in the unknown but also the demons of his own making. Jamie's quest for survival becomes a journey of redemption, where the chance for a new beginning is earned through courage, trust, and the willingness to face the truth of his own heart.

Luke Smith (4338.204.1 - 4338.209.2)

Luke Smith's world transforms with the discovery of a cryptic device, thrusting him into the guardianship of destiny itself. His charismatic charm and unpredictable decisions now carry weight beyond imagination, balancing on the razor's edge between salvation and destruction. Embracing his role as a Guardian, Luke faces the paradox of power: the very force that defends also threatens to annihilate. As shadows gather and the fabric of reality strains, Luke must navigate the consequences of his actions, unaware that a looming challenge will test the very core of his resolve.

4338.209.1 - 4338.214.1

KARL JENKINS

CLIVILIUS
WHERE CREATION MEETS INFINITY

"The line between obsession and dedication is often blurred, especially when it comes to solving a case that haunts you."

- Karl Jenkins

4338.209

(28 July 2018)

THE OPPORTUNITY

4338.209.1

"Oh my God, Jargus! What the hell happened last night?" I groaned, my voice a gritty rasp as I rolled over to look at my companion. My head was throbbing, a relentless reminder of the raucous night before. It wasn't out of the ordinary for me to grab a few drinks with colleagues at Salamanca. But last night, well, it had escalated quickly. Shots had lined the bar, and I, caught in the tidal wave of celebration, had hit them hard, each one a fiery testament to the night's significance.

After all, I'd just nailed my senior detective exam. Not just passed it, but aced it, earning me a well-deserved promotion and a transfer to the Major Crimes Unit. This wasn't just a step up the career ladder; it was a leap. And with this promotion came a tantalising promise: keep up my performance for the few next years, and I could be looking at sergeant stripes. That was indeed a cause for celebration, and celebrate we did, in true, unrestrained fashion.

The group of officers and detectives, my comrades in the field, had rallied around me, their voices loud and jovial, toasting to my success well into the early hours. I wasn't sure why I let it go so far, especially considering I had to be at work again soon. But as I lay there, staring at the ceiling with my temples pounding in sync with my heartbeat, I figured there was little point in dwelling on it. Gatorade and something greasy - that was the remedy I needed.

Beside me, Jargus hadn't moved an inch. He was crammed up against my side, his warm presence a comforting constant. I looked down at him, a gentle poke on his head eliciting a muffled whimper. Slowly, Jargus, my young German Shepherd, opened his eyes to squint back at me. His usually sharp, attentive gaze was dulled, a clear sign he was feeling the effects of last night too.

"You too, huh?" I said with a chuckle, my fingers finding their way to his head, scratching lightly. Jargus was more than just a pet; he was my loyal partner, always by my side. And he had good reason to be just as proud as I was. He was on his way to his own kind of promotion.

Jargus was no ordinary dog. Even as a young German Shepherd, he showed signs of incredible intelligence and ability, a real over-achiever among his pack of police dogs. His training was progressing at an impressive pace, already surpassing those many years his senior. He was, without a doubt, a remarkably talented dog. Lying there, looking at him, I couldn't help but feel a swell of pride for my young companion. We were both on our way up, and last night was just the beginning.

"We need to get up," I groaned, nudging Jargus with my knee. My voice was heavy, laden with the weight of last night's excesses, and my body felt like it was filled with lead. The room was still dim, the curtains drawn tight against the morning light, creating a cocoon of semi-darkness.

Jargus lifted his head slowly, his eyes meeting mine. There was a look in them, a blend of adoration and annoyance, that only a dog who's been woken prematurely could muster. His gaze was almost human in its expression, reflecting a mix of loyalty and mild irritation at being disturbed from his comfortable spot.

"Come on then," I repeated, nudging him a bit more firmly this time. My voice was a mix of coaxing and command, the tone I'd used countless times in our training sessions.

Jargus gave the room a slow, methodical sweep with his eyes. I could almost see the wheels turning in his head, his comprehensive training kicking in as he scanned for any sign of food or an opportunity for play. But the room was still, the remnants of last night's festivities offering neither. With a soft huff that seemed to convey his disappointment, he dropped his chin back to his paws.

"Fine, you lazy pup," I said with a chuckle, reaching out to scratch his head. His fur was soft under my fingers, a small comfort as I prepared to face the consequences of the night before.

I made an attempt to wriggle out of bed, envisioning a graceful, athletic leap to my feet. But reality had other plans. My legs, uncooperative and seemingly disconnected from my brain's commands, resulted in a clumsy tumble. I landed on the floor with a thud, my body sprawled in an unceremonious heap. It was far from the gazelle-like elegance I'd imagined.

Grimacing, I reached out to push myself up, my hand bracing against the bedside table for support. That's when I felt it - something slimy and sticky under my palm. "Eeew!" I exclaimed in revulsion, lifting my hand to inspect the source of the unpleasant sensation. Dangling from my outstretched palm was a used condom, its contents oozing onto the carpet with a consistency that reminded me unpleasantly of three-day-old rice pudding. The thing clung to my hand with a stubbornness that seemed almost mocking.

My eyes widened in horror and disgust. "That had better not be mine," I mumbled, a frown creasing my forehead. I thought of Sarah, my detective partner whom I was also tentatively starting to see more outside the office. We hadn't made anything official yet, but I had resolved to focus all my romantic energies on her. Despite my reputation, I was genuinely trying to give this monogamy thing a fair shot.

But then, a troubling thought struck me. If this condom wasn't mine, then whose was it? Sarah hadn't been with me last night, and I was fairly certain I hadn't brought anyone home. The pieces weren't adding up.

"This isn't yours, is it Jargus?" I turned to face the dog, holding up the incriminating evidence as if I were a lawyer in a courtroom drama. Jargus looked back at me, his head cocked in a bemused expression. He seemed to ponder the question, his canine brain trying to decipher the oddity I presented. But eventually, finding no logical answer in his doggy understanding, he let his head fall back onto the blanket, resigning himself to the comforts of his soft bed.

I frowned. A vague scene of hot, sweaty bodies bumping against each other in the cramped club, dancing to obnoxiously pounding bass flashed across my mind. I remembered the exhilaration I felt at a woman's hand touching my bare, trimmed chest, gliding her fingers admiringly over my rippling body. But the partial memory refused to reveal any face or name of the admirer.

At first, the nausea was just a slightly acidic taste in my mouth, a subtle but unwelcome reminder of last night's excesses. My tongue felt thick and cottony, as if it was coated in a layer of dust, and my throat was parched, each swallow a gritty endeavour. But this initial discomfort was just the prelude to a more severe storm brewing within.

Very quickly, my hangover escalated into full-blown agony. Stomach cramps gripped me like a vice, each wave more intense than the last. I could feel the bile, hot and acidic, clawing its way up my throat. It was a familiar routine, one I had endured more times than I cared to remember, yet each occurrence felt like a brutal new experience. As if on autopilot, my body knew what to do. I found myself racing for the bathroom, propelled by the urgent need to rid myself of the poison churning inside.

After reaching the sanctuary of the toilet, I succumbed to several deep heaves. Each one wracked my body, purging me of substances I didn't even recall consuming. The sounds and sensations were grotesque, a humiliating testament to the previous night's indulgences. This was followed by a few shorter, but no less intense, dry reaches into the toilet bowl. Gradually, as the last of the spasms subsided, my stomach began to ease, settling into a dull, lingering ache.

Without further delay, I nakedly crawled away from the gruesome Jackson Pollock study I had inadvertently created. The cold floor was a harsh contrast to my heated skin as I made my way to the shower. Reaching out with a shaky hand, I turned on the water, not caring for the temperature. I just needed to wash away the remnants of the night, both physically and metaphorically.

I sat there under the shower, my back flat against the cool tiles, which offered a small respite from the heat radiating from my body. The warmth of the water cascaded over me, splashing gently across my aching limbs and soothing the relentless pounding in my head. It felt like a small mercy in a morning filled with regrets.

My eyelids grew heavy, each blink an effort to keep the world in focus. My mind, foggy and uncooperative, struggled to latch onto any coherent thought for more than a fleeting moment. It was a losing battle, one where consciousness slipped away like sand through my fingers. Slowly, I drifted into a dark, pulsating world, a turbulent sea of strobed darkness where unwelcome memories lurked just beneath the surface, waiting to be awakened.

❖

My eyes snapped open with a sudden, jolting jerk. Confusion swirled in my mind as I scuttled across the slick, tiled floor of the shower, hastily reaching for the knob to shut off the water. The stream that had been soothingly warm only moments ago—or perhaps longer—had turned icy, sending shivers coursing through my body. I was freezing, the once comforting cocoon of warmth now replaced by an unforgiving chill. It was a harsh awakening; the hot water had evidently run its course during my unintended slumber, leaving me enveloped in coldness.

"Shit!" I muttered to myself, a shiver rattling my voice. Glancing down, I noticed my hands had become shrivelled prunes under the relentless assault of water. But more worryingly, as my gaze travelled further down, I realised with a mixture of amusement and concern that other parts of my body had also taken on the likeness of a small, wrinkled plum. A wry thought crossed my mind, *Surely I haven't been in here that long!*

With a groan, I forced myself to stand, muscles complaining at the sudden movement. Clambering out of the shower, I reached instinctively for a towel, only to grasp at empty air.

"Jargus, I need a towel!" I called out, my voice carrying a tone of instruction rather than desperation. True to his training and loyalty, within a minute Jargus appeared in the bathroom doorway. The sight of him, a fresh, grey towel hanging from his mouth, was both heartwarming and comical. "Thank you, Jargus," I said, a smile touching my lips despite the chill, as I carefully took the towel from him.

As I vigorously dried myself off, trying to rub some warmth back into my skin, the familiar ring of my phone echoed from the bedroom. "Shit," I swore again, a sense of urgency replacing the earlier disorientation.

Not bothering to wrap the towel around my still dripping and shivering body, I dashed into the bedroom. My wet footprints marked a clear path on the floor, a testament to my hasty retreat from the shower. Fumbling through the disarray of bedsheets and covers, I searched frantically for the phone, half-expecting it to be buried under the chaos of last night. To my surprise, and somewhat to the credit of Drunk Karl, the phone was sitting in plain sight on the side table. It seemed that, for once, my inebriated self had shown a hint of orderliness.

Reaching over, I grabbed the phone just in the nick of time, barely preventing it from rolling over to voicemail. My hand, still damp from the shower, left a wet imprint on the device as I held it to my ear, bracing myself for whatever the call might bring.

"Yeah," I answered, my voice coming out in a croak. I tried to inject a tone of sobriety into my words, an effort that fell embarrassingly short. The room swayed slightly, and I braced myself against the bedside table for support.

"Where the hell are you, Karl?" The voice on the other end was sharp, laced with panic and barely contained frustration. I recognised it immediately: Sarah, her usually calm demeanour replaced by a palpable sense of urgency.

"I'm still at home. The alarm didn't go off," I replied, my words slurring slightly despite my best efforts to sound convincing. It was a feeble excuse, and I knew it.

"Bullshit," she shot back. The disbelief in her voice was clear, cutting through my foggy brain. "I know you went out with the boys last night."

I sighed, a heavy, defeated sound. Closing my eyes, I pinched the bridge of my nose, feeling the embarrassment wash over me. This was not how I had imagined starting my first official day as a senior detective. "What is it, Sarah?" I asked, forcing myself to focus on her words, to push past the hangover that clung to me like a second skin.

"You need to get your ass down to the station right now," she said, her tone brooking no argument.

"Can't it wait until later?" I groaned, the thought of moving, of facing the world outside my bedroom, seeming like an insurmountable task.

"No, Karl. It can't. This could be your big case." Her words pierced through the haze, carrying a weight that momentarily sobered me.

I paused for a few moments, the gravity of her words slowly sinking in. My mind, still clouded by the remnants of alcohol, struggled to process the information, to shift from the chaos of the night before to the reality of my responsibilities. "Fine. I'll be there in half an hour," I promised, the words more a declaration to myself than to her.

Ending the call abruptly, I stood there for a moment, phone still in hand, as the reality of the situation began to crystallise. This was it – the big case, the kind that could define a career. And here I was, barely able to stand straight, a poor start to what was supposed to be a pivotal day in my career. I shook my head, a mix of frustration and resolve settling over me. *Time to pull myself together*, I thought, casting one last glance at the disorder around me before preparing to face the day.

THE INTERVIEW

4338.209.2

I savoured the last moment of hot water before turning off the taps. I had successfully snuck into the station without anyone noticing that I had arrived and headed straight to the showers to enjoy the warmth I had been denied earlier.

"Shit, Sarah!" I said as I pulled back the cheap plastic shower curtain. "What the fuck are you doing in here?"

"Looking for some action, I'd say," Glen taunted, grinning as he braced himself against the doorway to the changing rooms, wearing only a towel around his waist. He pushed his overweight body past Sarah, purposely brushing his hairy potbelly against her arm. The towel that only just fit around his considerable girth dropped to the floor, and he stepped into the cramped cubicle next to me. Glen paused for a moment, exposing his full-frontal nudity before pulling the curtain across.

"In your dreams, pal," I called out to him.

"Ew, please no. Don't encourage that fat prick," said Sarah, clearly grossed out by the suggestion of making a cameo in one of Glen's distasteful erotic dreams that he so freely recounted, in nauseating detail, around the office.

I started to feel the coldness that I had been trying to vanquish seep slowly back into my bones. "Towel," I directed Sarah, indicating to where my things were piled up on the bench in front of the shower.

She reached out and quickly grabbed the white towel, clearly wanting to get going with something. "Hurry up, you'll want to hear this," she said, shoving the towel at my carefully buzzed, but still furry, chest.

The three other officers and I in the changing room, didn't make any attempt to disguise our staring at Sarah's firm butt as she walked past the row of lockers and out through the doorway into the corridor. My hungry gaze lingered on the closed door until the slight thud of a cake of soap falling to the bottom of the shower next to me broke my trance. I watched as the soap slid out from under the curtain, stopping near my feet.

"Piss off, Glen," I said as I walked to my locker, leaving the soap where it lay. Glen let out a hearty chuckle, which echoed out of his cubicle and around the changing room. I found it so creepy, it made my freshly clean skin feel dirty again. Glen really was such a pervert that he was almost a caricature. It was ridiculous. *If he ever laid a finger on Sarah...*

"Glen again?" Sergeant Charlie Claiborne asked, standing over me and interrupting my idle thought of beating Glen to within an inch of his life.

"He's all yours, Sergeant," I offered.

"Get your clothes on, Detective Jenkins. Detective Lahey is right. You're going to want to hear what this woman has to say," Sergeant Claiborne said sternly as he turned to leave the room. He strode purposefully away, before stopping dead in his tracks outside the cubicle in which Glen was showering. He paused for a moment, seemingly in thought, before rapping hard on the cubicle wall, eliciting an amusing squeal of surprise from its occupant.

"Detective?" he called out, with an air of authority that superior officers seemed to affect as they climbed the hierarchy.

"Yes, Sergeant?" came Glen's meek reply.

"You have precisely two minutes to get your ass parked at your desk or so help me it will be graveyard shifts for the rest of the week. Understood?" barked Claiborne, turning to smile ever so slightly in my direction.

He must have overheard Glen being a dick, I thought, grinning wryly back at my boss. *Serves him right.*

"Y-Y-Yes, sir!" stammered Glen, as frantic scrubbing sounds began emanating from his cubicle.

"Now hurry up, Jenkins," the Sergeant said to me, as he walked quickly out of the changing rooms. "I wanted you in that interview room ten minutes ago."

Slowly, I leaned forward as the Sergeant disappeared around the corner, resting my still slightly sore forehead on the top of the metal locker's frame. *Why today?* I asked myself pitifully. Hastily pulling my clothes on, I watched in amusement as Glen tried to dry himself in three seconds flat. As Glen rushed out of the changing rooms, belly rolls visibly wobbling, still dripping wet with traces of shampoo in his hair, I swallowed a couple of headache tablets and prayed to any god that was listening that I'd be able to focus enough despite my hangover to actually get through the shift.

❖

I walked the full length of the corridor, each step feeling heavier than the last. My mind was a whirlwind of thoughts, still trying to latch onto the seriousness of the situation. The corridor seemed longer than usual, the familiar sights and sounds of the station now distant and muffled, as if I was moving through water.

Stopping outside the interview room, I saw the Sergeant waiting. Sarah was there too, her impatience palpable. She tapped her pen against a pad rhythmically, a clear sign of her eagerness to get things underway. The sound was like a metronome, ticking away the seconds, each tap a reminder of the urgency and my own unpreparedness.

"She's in there," Sarah said, her voice firm, leaving no room for doubt or hesitation. She steered me closer to the door, her hand on my arm guiding yet assertive. "You ready for this?" There was a challenge in her eyes, a silent questioning of my capability in that moment.

I nodded in response, more out of reflex than confidence. My throat felt dry, and my head still pounded. As I moved towards the interview room door, bracing myself for what lay ahead, the Sergeant suddenly intervened.

His hand slammed hard into my chest, a sudden and unexpected barrier. The force of it knocked the breath out of me, halting my advance abruptly. I stood there, stunned and gasping for air, a mix of surprise and unease washing over me. The Sergeant's eyes bore into mine, examining each carefully in turn. His gaze was piercing, searching, as if trying to gauge my readiness, or lack thereof.

"I'd normally tell you to go home," the Sergeant said, his voice firm and unyielding. "But she has a unique story to tell, and she's determined to tell it to you, specifically." There was a gravity in his words, a seriousness that underscored the importance of what was about to unfold.

The Sergeant removed his hand, and his next words were a clear directive. "Now, don't screw it up." The weight of his expectation hung heavily in the air.

Nervously, I swallowed hard, the bile in my throat a harsh reminder of my physical state.

"I'll be watching you closely," the Sergeant added, his glare sharp and dangerous. Any humour that might have come from the usual banter with Glen was now completely absent. This was serious, and the stakes were high.

I knew the gravity of the situation. If I messed this up, it wouldn't just be my promotion on the line – it could be the very trajectory of my career. Taking a deep, steadying breath, I tried to calm the storm of nerves raging inside me.

Detective Lahey opened the door to the interview room, and we filed inside, one after the other. I stepped into the room, acutely aware of the Sergeant's eyes on me, the weight of the responsibility I was about to shoulder pressing down. It was time to prove myself, not just as a senior detective, but as someone worthy of the trust and expectations placed upon me.

"Louise Jeffries?" The words left my mouth in a mix of disbelief and surprise as I took in the sight of the woman sitting at the interview desk. The years had etched new lines onto her face, lines that spoke of hardships and sleepless nights. Her expression was solemn, almost haunting, as if she carried a weight far too heavy for one person to bear. She didn't speak, but the silence between us was loud, filled with unspoken words and memories.

"Oh my God! It is you," I couldn't help but exclaim, my voice tinged with a sense of incredulity. The last time I saw Louise, years seemed to have been a lifetime ago, in a past that now felt both distant and painfully close.

"You two know each other?" Sarah's voice cut through my thoughts, snapping me back to the present.

"You could say that," I answered, my voice a soft murmur. Memories of Louise and me, from a time long gone, flickered in my mind like old film reels. "How have you been?" I asked her, though the question felt hollow against the backdrop of her pained expression.

Louise's face remained unchanged, her features set in a mask of quiet resolve. "Please, Karl. Sit," she insisted, her voice steady yet carrying an undercurrent of urgency.

A sense of dread began to creep into my stomach, an ominous feeling that grew with every passing second. I pulled up the chair opposite her and sat down, my movements mechanical, driven by a growing apprehension.

"I've already told most of this to your colleague here," Louise said, nodding towards Sarah. "But I wanted to tell you directly." Her voice was steady, but I could sense the effort it took her to maintain that composure.

A cool gust from the air conditioning unit swept through the room, sending a shiver down my spine. The chill seemed to accentuate the gravity of the moment, heightening the tension that hung in the air.

"I'm listening," I said, striving to keep my tone serious, to maintain a professional demeanour despite the turmoil brewing inside me. My eyes locked with Louise's, urging her to continue. I was acutely aware of how my emotions might be betraying me, the concern and anxiety likely evident in my gaze.

Louise's gaze held mine with a directness that was both familiar and unsettling. The intensity in her eyes spoke volumes, reflecting a turmoil of emotions. As she paused, a weary sigh escaped her lips, betraying the effort it took her to maintain composure. The news she was about to deliver hung heavily in the air, a foreboding sense that it would alter the course of things. "My son, Kain, is missing."

The mention of Kain sent a flicker of memory through my mind. I vaguely remembered him – a young boy with a well-set frame, honed from years of high school football. His youthful face, marked by the innocence of adolescence, now seemed to loom in my thoughts. I recalled the time when Louise had come to me, desperate for help after Kain got caught underage drinking. I had pulled some strings back then, a small gesture of repayment for the countless ways Louise had been there for me in the past. A wave of unease washed over me at the thought that she might have revealed our past dealings to Sarah... about everything. But as I studied Louise's face, her efforts to keep her emotions in check apparent, I realised she hadn't said anything. Our secret remained just that.

"And so is my brother," she added after a long, heavy pause.

"Jamie?" The name came out cautiously from my lips. Jamie – her brother, another figure from my past, who had moved back to Tasmania thirteen years ago. Despite the occasional sightings around town, we hadn't spoken since that fateful day – a day etched in my memory with a mix of regret and unresolved questions.

"Yes," Louise nodded, confirming my fears.

"Are you sure?" I pressed. My voice was steady, but inside, a storm of emotions raged. Jamie's disappearance wasn't just another case. It was personal, deeply intertwined with a past that never seemed to let go. We may not have spoken for nearly two decades, but the mystery surrounding Jamie, the cause of his fear, had never ceased to haunt me. It had torn apart a bond of fellowship, a connection that I hadn't been able to replicate with anyone else since. The thought that something might have happened to him reignited a sense of duty and urgency within me, a need to uncover the truth that had been left buried for too long.

"I haven't been able to contact him for several days now. He hasn't answered any of my calls or responded to any of my texts. I've driven past his house a few times and his car is still in the driveway," Louise's voice trembled slightly as she explained, her words painting a picture of growing desperation and concern. The thought of Jamie, once so integral to my life, now possibly in trouble, sent a jolt of anxiety through me.

"Have you knocked on the door?" I asked, my forehead creasing with worry. It struck me as odd that she would only drive past without attempting to make direct contact.

"I didn't at first," she replied, her eyes welling up with tears. "Maybe if I had, Kain would still be around." Her voice broke as she wiped her eyes with the back of her hand, the gesture one of frustration and regret.

"I'm confused, Louise. You said you didn't knock on his door at first. But you have now?" I needed her to clarify, to understand the sequence of events. My mind was already racing, trying to piece together the scant information, to form a starting point for the investigation.

"Yes," she confessed, her voice barely above a whisper. "But he didn't answer. I only spoke to Luke."

"Who is Luke?" I interjected, a frown settling on my face. The name didn't ring any bells, and it felt like a crucial piece of information I was missing.

"Luke Smith," Louise said, pausing as if the name held a significant weight. "Jamie's partner."

"Oh. I didn't realise," I admitted, feeling a pang of surprise. How had I not known about Jamie's partner? We had been so close back then, practically inseparable. It was disconcerting to realise how much had changed, how distant I had become from a young man who had once been my closest confidant.

"It's okay," Louise's voice carried a tone of understanding, perhaps even forgiveness, for my ignorance about Jamie's life. Her words offered a small comfort, but my mind had already shifted gears, moving past personal embarrassments and focusing on the unfolding situation.

I took a deep breath, feeling the weight of responsibility settle on my shoulders. I needed to piece together the scattered fragments of information, to form a coherent picture of what had happened. "Louise," I began slowly, deliberately. "I'm still quite confused. Please, start again from the beginning," I requested, my voice steady, yet filled with urgency.

"The beginning?" Louise echoed, her eyebrows knitting together in surprise.

"Just of the disappearance," I quickly clarified. The last thing I wanted was for her to delve into the history of twenty years ago. That was a chapter of my life I wasn't ready to revisit, not here, not now. Or ever, for that matter.

Louise took a deep breath, her chest rising and falling as she gathered her thoughts. "It's been four days since I've been able to get in touch with Jamie, and it's unusual that he doesn't answer my calls. I'm concerned about his relationship with Luke, so I sent Kain over to their house to check on him. But I haven't heard from Kain since."

As she spoke, I could see the struggle on her face, the effort it took to keep her emotions in check. Her lower lip trembled, a physical manifestation of the fear and worry that gripped her.

"I'm really worried that something terrible might have happened to them," Louise said, her voice strained as she fought back tears. The vulnerability in her eyes was palpable, the glimmer of unshed tears reflecting the room's dim light.

Moved by Louise's evident distress, I reached across the small interview table, my hand enveloping her trembling ones. It was a gesture meant to offer comfort, a tangible expression of support in a moment charged with fear and uncertainty. "When did you send Kain?" I asked, my voice soft yet underscored with the insistence of a detective needing vital information.

"Two days ago. It was first thing in the morning," she replied, her voice barely above a whisper. "I've contacted Kain's friends, but nobody has seen or heard from him since he left our house. Kain's fiancé swears to me she hasn't heard from him either." Her words painted a picture of a widening circle of worry, a network of people touched by Kain's unexplained absence.

"So, after driving past Jamie's house several times, I finally decided yesterday morning—" Her voice hitched, choked by the emotions she had been battling to keep at bay. I felt her hands tremble more violently under my grasp. Squeezing them gently, I tried to offer reassurance, my own mind racing with questions and theories. I needed to hear the rest, to understand the full scope of what we were dealing with.

"I decided," Louise continued after a moment, gathering herself with visible effort, "That I'd go and knock on the door. I pulled into the driveway, but I didn't get a chance to knock. Luke was already walking out the front door." Her recounting of these details was methodical, each word laced with the weight of her worry.

"I asked him about Jamie, and he told me that they were having relationship issues and he had gone to Melbourne for a few weeks to think things over." The revelation added another layer of complexity to the case. Jamie and Luke's relationship problems, Jamie's sudden trip to Melbourne, it all seemed to weave a complicated web around the disappearances.

I sat back slightly, the chair creaking under my weight as I processed the deluge of information Louise had just provided. My mind was racing, trying to connect the dots, to make sense of the jumbled timelines and tangled relationships. Kain's mysterious disappearance, Jamie's sudden and unexplained departure, their intertwined lives with Louise - it all seemed like disparate pieces of a puzzle that refused to align.

"And do you believe him?" I asked, my voice carrying a mixture of skepticism and concern. This was a critical question. The reliability of Luke's account was paramount in determining the next steps of the investigation.

"Well, he did seem to be pretty upset about it all," Louise replied, her voice tinged with doubt. "But even if it were true and Jamie had gone to Melbourne, that doesn't explain why he won't respond to any of my calls or messages."

"And did Luke say anything about Kain?" I pressed further, needing every fragment of information, no matter how small or seemingly insignificant.

"Not really. He just said that Kain never made it around. He said he hadn't seen him since last Christmas."

"None of this makes any sense at all," Detective Lahey suddenly interjected, breaking her silence. I realised then that in the intensity of my focus on Louise's story, I had almost forgotten about Sarah's presence in the room.

"No, it doesn't," I agreed with her, my thoughts already shifting to the next steps we needed to take. Standing up, I motioned for Louise to follow suit. "Thank you for coming in, Louise," I said, my tone professional yet empathetic. "Detective Lahey and I will write up our notes and open an investigation immediately. We'll keep you informed of our progress. I'm sure we'll be in touch very soon."

"Thank you, Karl," Louise said, her voice cracking slightly with emotion. Our eyes met, and for a fleeting moment, a torrent of shared history passed between us. I could feel my heart pounding, a stark reminder to keep my emotions in check. I had to focus on the task at hand – finding Jamie and Kain.

"Detective Lahey will take you to a more comfortable room where you can write up your formal statement," I continued, maintaining a steady voice despite the turmoil inside me.

Louise cast a quick glance at Sarah, then back at me, her expression slightly rolling her eyes, clearly not thrilled at the prospect of recounting everything again to someone she didn't know.

A twinge of guilt added to the burden I was already carrying. I placed a reassuring hand on Louise's shoulder.

"Don't worry," I said firmly, trying to infuse confidence into my words. "We'll find them. Both of them."

She gave a slight nod, her expression a mix of gratitude and worry. I watched sombrely as Detective Lahey escorted her out of the room, my mind already turning over the possibilities, the leads we had to follow, the questions that needed answering.

❖

As soon as the room emptied, the Sergeant strode in with a brisk, purposeful gait, his presence filling the space with an air of authority. "So, what do you think of her story?" he asked, his voice carrying a note of skepticism. "Do you believe any of it?"

I found myself in a quandary, caught between my professional duties and the personal connections entangling me in this case. *I have to tread carefully,* I reminded myself, aware that every word, every reaction could be scrutinised. I shrugged noncommittally. "I don't know. It doesn't really make much sense at the moment." I paused, weighing my next words. "I'll do a background check on Luke Smith. See if I can find any connection with–" I stopped abruptly, cutting off the sentence before I ventured into territory that might be premature to discuss.

The Sergeant's eyes bore into me, scrutinising, searching for something unsaid. "I agree," he responded, his gaze unwavering. "You sure you don't think you're too close to this one, Jenkins?" His question caught me off guard, a jolt of alarm shooting through me.

Shit! Does he know? The thought was like a shockwave, sending my mind into overdrive. *How could he know about my past with Jamie? It was impossible, wasn't it? We hadn't been in Tasmania back then, and I was certain no official record existed of those days long gone.*

Eager to escape the weight of his gaze, I took a step toward the door. The Sergeant's probing eyes and pointed questions were becoming too much, igniting a storm of anxiety within me. I needed space, time to organise my thoughts, to separate them from the emotions swirling dangerously close to the surface. *After all,* I reminded myself, *I am Hobart's newest senior detective. I have to get this right.*

"Be careful, Karl. These are dangerous times, and we have to deal with dangerous people," the Sergeant said, his voice low and measured. He extended his hand, clenched into a fist. My eyes fixed on his hand, a sense of foreboding growing within me.

Slowly, Sergeant Claiborne unfurled his fingers, revealing a small, torn, scrunched up piece of scrap paper. My heart skipped a beat as I recognised it, a flood of memories rushing back.

"Does Louise know?" I managed to ask, my voice strained as I struggled to keep the panic at bay.

"No," he replied softly, his head shaking slowly. The Sergeant's subtle actions and the appearance of the scrap paper left me reeling.

THE INVESTIGATION BEGINS

4338.209.3

Sarah's voice cut through the haze of my thoughts, grounding me back in the present. "Where do you want to start this investigation?" she asked, her tone business-like yet tinged with a hint of curiosity.

I rose from the shabby chair that had become too familiar over the years, its worn fabric a testament to the countless hours spent pondering over cases. Moving towards the wall behind me, I eyed the single piece of butcher's paper that I had stuck there amidst a collage of notes, pictures, and files – a makeshift tapestry of investigation.

"I've been putting a bit of a timeline together," I said, my voice tinged with thoughtfulness. The timeline was a crude yet necessary tool, a way to visually piece together the fragmented events as we understood them.

"On that?" Sarah's question came with a raised eyebrow, her gaze shifting between me and the butcher's paper.

"What?" I shrugged nonchalantly, feeling a slight defensive edge creep into my voice. "I wanted to get my thoughts out before they disappeared." In this line of work, every detail mattered, and the fear of losing a crucial piece of information was always lurking in the back of my mind.

"Oh, come on, Senior Detective," Sarah replied, her grin spreading across her face. Her teasing tone was familiar, a welcome respite in the midst of tension. "Give yourself a little more credit."

I couldn't help but return her smile, feeling a momentary lift from the growing burden on my shoulders. Sarah's lighthearted humour was like a beacon in the often murky waters of police work. Despite the gravity of our current case, her presence brought a semblance of normalcy, a reminder of the world outside these walls.

Our relationship, whatever it might be called, was an enigma even to me. We spent countless hours together, both in the precinct and out, yet there was an unspoken agreement between us. Neither of us had rushed to define what we were, and honestly, that worked for me. In a job where uncertainties were the only certainty, the undefined nature of our relationship was oddly comforting. It was one less pressure to contend with, one less expectation to meet.

"So, what have you timelined then?" Sarah's question brought me back to the task at hand, her curiosity evident in her tone.

"Not a lot," I confessed, my gaze returning to the wall that had become a makeshift canvas for the investigation. The array of events, crudely represented, seemed almost juvenile in their simplicity. "We know that this," I said, pointing to a rudimentary stick figure I'd drawn. It was skinny-headed, armless, more a child's doodle than anything else. "Was the last time Louise heard from her brother." The figure stood alone, a solitary marker in a timeline that felt increasingly complex.

"This second figure, further along, is when she sent Kain to check on them." I traced my finger along an imaginary line to another stick figure, this one slightly closer to the present marker on my timeline.

"And the third one?" Sarah's voice pulled me further along the timeline.

"That's Louise coming to visit us today," I answered, slightly surprised that it wasn't immediately obvious. *Sure, my artistic skills were lacking, but the context*, I thought, *should have filled in the gaps.*

"Of course," Sarah said, a hint of embarrassment colouring her voice as she caught on.

I paused, my mind whirling with the possibilities that lay ahead. Scenarios, each with its own set of outcomes and implications, raced through my head. Despite my less-than-stellar drawing skills, my analytical abilities were sharp. It was my capacity to juggle multiple theories, to sift through the noise and find the signal, that had propelled me to my current position. *My competence*, I reassured myself, *was not in question.*

"We should start by checking their bank accounts," I decided abruptly. It was a starting point, a way to anchor the investigation in something concrete. With that thought, I pivoted on my heels and set off to initiate the process. No further words were necessary; the situation urged me forward, my mind already racing ahead to the next steps, to the untangling of this intricate web we found ourselves in.

❖

Having gained access to both Jamie and Kain's financial records, a feat made more challenging by the less-than-cooperative bank manager, Sarah and I divided the task. She delved into Jamie's accounts, her eyes scanning each line with precision, while I began combing through Kain's records. I quickly realised that Kain's financial activity was unremarkable. He still lived at home, and his bank records reflected a routine of a young man not yet burdened by major financial responsibilities. Fuel consumption, occasional grocery purchases, and a few personal indulgences - nothing that raised any red flags. However, one detail stood out starkly: his account had been dormant since the night before Louise claimed she had sent him to check on Jamie.

I glanced across the table at Sarah, feeling a mix of frustration and concern. Her attention was entirely absorbed by Jamie's bank statements, her forehead creased in concentration. "Well, that was a fruitless exercise," I sighed, leaning back in my chair. The lack of any significant findings in Kain's financial records only deepened the mystery.

Sarah continued her meticulous examination, seemingly unfazed by my comment. I pressed on, sharing my thoughts aloud, "Unless Kain has additional investments and finances secretly stashed elsewhere, which I highly doubt given how generous his parents seem to be, he has very simple spending habits and, frankly, not much money. There's no indication that he purchased plane tickets or jumped on the ferry to Melbourne. But–"

At that moment, Sarah's head snapped up, her focus instantly shifting to me. "But?" she queried, her tone sharp with interest.

"Looks like Kain is a fan of Candy Crush. There are a few small transactions from the game at around 11:00 P.M. on the night before he visited Jamie, but I don't see how that's going to help us determine what happened after he saw Jamie. If he ever did see him, that is." I leaned back, my hands intertwined behind my head, feeling the weight of unanswered questions.

"You don't think he did?" Sarah's question cut through my thoughts, her voice laced with a mix of surprise and skepticism.

"I'm not sure yet," I admitted, my eyes drifting towards the ceiling as I contemplated the myriad possibilities. The uncertainty was gnawing at me, each unturned stone in this investigation adding to the growing sense of unease.

I sat in contemplative silence, lost in the labyrinth of my thoughts, while Sarah finished poring over Jamie's accounts.

The sound of rustling papers filled the air, a rhythmic accompaniment to the ticking of the clock on the wall.

Suddenly, Sarah broke the silence with a hint of triumph in her voice. "Well, I might have something." She reached the end of the bank statements and thrust the final piece of paper towards me. "There. Look at the last transaction," she urged, her finger jabbing at a specific line on the page.

I leaned forward, my eyes scanning the details. "Possibly," I murmured, nodding slightly, though skepticism still clouded my judgment.

"Possibly?" Sarah echoed, her voice rising in disbelief. "Only possibly? This is huge!" she exclaimed, her enthusiasm a sharp contrast to my cautious skepticism.

"But it doesn't prove anything or give us any real information," I pointed out, trying to temper her excitement with a dose of reality.

"He totally drained his bank account in a single transaction three days ago," Sarah countered, her eyes locked on mine, conveying the gravity of her discovery. "Louise is clearly justified in suspecting some sort of foul play."

Inside, I could feel a simmering frustration. Sarah was a competent detective, no question, but her eagerness sometimes overshadowed the need for thorough analysis. In this line of work, jumping to conclusions could be a dangerous game. It was critical to consider all avenues, to follow the evidence meticulously, not to let it be swayed by personal biases or hasty judgments.

"I reckon that Luke Smith killed Jamie, then Kain caught him covering up the body, so Luke killed him, too," Sarah ventured, her voice tinged with a mix of excitement and certainty. Her enthusiasm was understandable; this could potentially be her first major homicide investigation. But her haste in drawing conclusions was concerning. And my own headache, throbbing relentlessly, wasn't helping me guide her with the patience I usually mustered.

"Sarah!" I snapped, more harshly than I intended. The urgency to temper her rush to judgment outweighed my usual restraint.

At my outburst, Sarah fell silent. I realised then that I had risen from my chair, standing now in the middle of the office, the focus of surrounding attention. The sudden quiet felt heavy, punctuated only by the distant hum of office activity. I felt the weight of the gazes upon me, the unspoken question in their eyes about my reaction.

I met their stares, unflinching, a firm resolve settling within me. This was more than just maintaining authority; it was about demonstrating the rigour and responsibility that my role as a senior detective demanded. I had earned my rank, not just through years of service but through countless hours of careful analysis, measured decisions, and the ability to keep a level head even in the most challenging of circumstances. And now I was determined to prove that I deserved my title.

As I stood there, surrounded by the familiar clutter of the office, my resolve solidified to meticulously piecing together a puzzle that seemed to grow more complex by the minute. My mind churned through the sparse information we had, attempting to form a cohesive narrative from the disjointed facts.

The evidence, as sparse as it was, could potentially align with Luke's – or rather, Louise's interpretation of Luke's – version of events. But that was speculative at best until we got Luke's own account. Jamie's financial moves were intriguing: emptying his savings, drawing out thousands from his credit card before Kain was supposed to visit him. If Jamie had that much cash on hand, it suggested he might be planning to lay low locally, avoiding detection and perhaps sidestepping his troubled relationship with Luke. His car, left behind yet easily retrievable, hinted at the possibility that he hadn't ventured far.

But the question that nagged at me was: why didn't Jamie take his car right away? *If Luke's story about their relationship woes and Jamie's supposed trip to Melbourne held any truth, then Jamie's actions seemed designed to convince Luke of his departure, buying him time to manage his affairs undisturbed. It was a clever ruse if true, but it raised more questions than it answered.*

Then there was Kain. *How did he fit into this puzzle? Was he an unwitting participant, or was he actively aiding Jamie in some way?*

"Aha!" The exclamation slipped from my lips unintentionally, a product of the gears turning in my head. I hardly noticed I'd spoken aloud until Sarah's response brought me back to the present.

"What?" she asked, her curiosity piqued.

Ignoring her question momentarily, I continued to unravel the threads in my mind. *Louise had mentioned Kain taking his ute, which was now also missing. It clicked in place. If Kain was assisting Jamie, then Jamie wouldn't need his own car immediately. They could use Kain's ute for whatever they were planning.*

"Sarah," I finally addressed her, my voice firm with newfound clarity. "If we can find Kain, he'll lead us straight to Jamie."

"Are you sure?" Her skepticism was evident, but I couldn't blame her. The pieces of this puzzle were fitting together in a pattern that only became clear after connecting the dots of years of experience.

"Jamie has all the skills to go off the grid if he wants to. That'll make him hard to pin down on our own. We need Kain. He's the one who can lead us to Jamie." As I spoke, a realisation dawned on me, a slight slip in my usually guarded demeanour. I had revealed more about Jamie than I should have known from the information gathered today. I quickly redirected the conversation, hoping Sarah hadn't caught on to my inadvertent slip.

"I don't think you're going to find anything, but if Jamie has that much cash, he could have purchased plane tickets without leaving a record. I want you to follow up with both the Hobart and Launceston airports to check whether either Jamie or Kain have boarded any flights in the last five days."

"Okay," she replied, her tone professional, yet I sensed a flicker of curiosity in her gaze.

"And when you're done with that, given Kain's ute is missing, go and check with the ferry service. There's a chance they could have made it to the mainland."

"I'm on it," Sarah responded, her nod filled with the enthusiasm that was a hallmark of her approach to detective work. "And what are you going to do?"

I paused for a moment, considering my next move. "I'm going to visit Luke Smith."

Sarah looked hurt, her expression shifting. "But—"

"Time is of the essence here, Sarah," I interjected, cutting her off. Her disappointment was palpable, but necessary decisions often came with a personal cost. "If my hunch is wrong and you're closer to the mark, then Jamie and Kain are in danger and we have to divide and conquer."

I knew Sarah well enough to anticipate her response. We usually conducted suspect interviews together, a routine that had become almost second nature. But this case was different, it demanded a split approach. Each lead, no matter how thin, needed to be pursued with diligence and urgency.

As I watched Sarah gather her materials, a sense of responsibility weighed heavily on me. Her readiness to dive into the investigation was evident, but my decision to keep her at arm's length from my thoughts about Jamie gnawed at my conscience. In this line of work, trust and transparency within a team were crucial, yet there were moments when instincts guided me down a solitary path. This was one of those moments.

I was still wrestling with the idea of any immediate danger to Jamie and Kain. The pieces of the puzzle hadn't yet aligned to form a clear picture of threat, but the unknowns were too significant to ignore. I needed some time alone, away from the buzz of the station, to process and reflect. My head was still throbbing from the night before, a relentless reminder of my own fallibility. I couldn't afford to let my guard down, not when every detail, every word could mean the difference between a breakthrough and a dead end.

In assigning tasks to Sarah, I ensured she would be engaged, her focus diverted. It was a tactical move, designed to give me the space I needed without arousing suspicion or concern. I trusted her capabilities, but in my current state, I couldn't risk revealing more than necessary. The tasks would keep her busy, and more importantly, safe.

"Fine," Sarah responded, her tone indicating acceptance but not without a hint of resignation. I could sense her desire to delve deeper, to be more involved, but she understood the necessity of our divided approach.

I let out a barely audible sigh of relief as I collected my thoughts. It was time to confront Luke Smith, to peel back the layers of his story and see what truths lay beneath. My coat felt heavy on my shoulders as I donned it, a physical manifestation of the burden of the investigation.

Right then, Mr. Smith, I thought determinedly, my steps quickening as I made my way out of the station. A sense of purpose leading me forward. It was time for a candid conversation with Luke, time to gather the missing pieces of this increasingly complex puzzle. The way he responded, the nuances in his expressions and words, could unlock the next phase of our investigation. This wasn't just about following protocol; it was about intuition, about reading between the lines to uncover the hidden truths. And I was ready to face whatever that entailed.

THE DISCOVERY

4338.209.4

Sitting in my car outside Luke's house, I switched off the engine and was enveloped in darkness. The quiet of the night surrounded me, punctuated only by the occasional distant sound of a car passing by. I had already been here once today, driven by an unshakeable need for answers, but left with nothing but disappointment. Luke hadn't answered the door. In fact, no one had. The house had remained silent, almost eerily so.

I had peered through the ground floor windows, the ones where the blinds weren't completely drawn shut, hoping for a glimpse of anything that might provide a clue. But my search had been in vain. All I saw were ordinary rooms, nothing that hinted at the turmoil possibly unfolding in the lives of its inhabitants.

The garbage bins underneath the kitchen window had caught my eye, filled to the brim, with several more bags piled up in the back bedroom. At the time, it hadn't struck me as particularly unusual; households generate waste, after all. But later, as I prepared dinner at home, the image of those black plastic bags resurfaced in my mind with sudden clarity. I'd only seen them through a narrow gap between almost closed blinds, but there were at least four, maybe five bags. *Why so much garbage?*

In a split-second decision, I turned off the stove, abandoning my half-prepared steak. I wrapped it in clingfilm and placed it back in the fridge. "Sorry, Jargus," I said to the dog, who sat by the kitchen bench, his tail wagging in hopeful expectation of a treat. I bent down and gave him a pat on the head, a poor substitute for the steak he had been eyeing. But tonight, my mind was elsewhere, fixated on the task at hand.

The garbage bags, the unanswered door, the silent house — they all pointed to something amiss. It was more than just a hunch; it was an itch that needed scratching, a puzzle that demanded solving. I had to return to Luke's house, to delve deeper, to look beyond the ordinary and find the extraordinary clues that might be hiding in plain sight. This was what being a detective was about — following your instincts, even when they led you back to the same place, looking for answers in the shadows. And tonight, those shadows beckoned from Luke's house.

❖

As I sat in my car along the quiet road behind Luke's house, the creek whispered through the wilderness on the other side, its gentle murmur a stark contrast to the silence that shrouded the house.

The first time I drove past, the house had been cloaked in complete darkness. Now, hours later, nothing had changed. It stood there, an enigmatic structure swallowed by the night. The darkness seemed almost tangible, like a thick, oppressive blanket that extinguished any hint of life within. The stillness of the house was unnerving, as if it was holding its breath, harbouring secrets in its shadowy depths.

As midnight struck, I decided it was time to take a closer look. I quietly opened the car door, carefully easing myself out to avoid any noise that might disturb the heavy silence. Standing beside the car, I let the cool night air wash over me, listening to the rustling of gum trees and the distant screeches of possums in the underbrush. Yet, the house remained dark, no lights flickering to life, no signs of movement. The darkness was absolute, unyielding.

Reaching for my phone, the sudden brightness of the screen jolted me, its glow a stark contrast to the encompassing darkness. My eyes adjusted, and I opened a new text message, my fingers hovering over the keypad. I began to type the name of the person I needed to contact: Jamie Gre—

The name stirred a torrent of mixed emotions within me. The stillness of the night seemed to amplify the internal conflict raging in my mind. *Was Jamie more deeply involved in this situation than I had initially thought? Was he a victim, or was the truth of his disappearance far more complicated than it appeared on the surface?* Standing alone in the darkness, I realised the gravity of the message I was about to send. This single text had the potential to untangle the twisted threads of the case, possibly shining a light on truths that were now shrouded in mystery.

With a deep breath, I readied myself to press 'send', but abruptly, my finger froze above the screen. A deluge of memories from Queensland suddenly overwhelmed me. I was taken back to my nineteenth birthday - a day marred by the absence of Jamie, my best mate. He never showed up to the party, and that absence had opened a chasm of unanswered questions and unspoken tensions between us.

Days later, the confrontation between us had been explosive. I had accused Jamie of hiding something from me, something potentially damaging, something that threatened the very foundation of our friendship. Jamie had vehemently denied my accusations, claiming he had been in hiding, paranoid and convinced that he was being watched. The argument had spiralled out of control, and in a moment of unchecked rage, I had struck him. The punch sent Jamie reeling over the edge of a small bridge and into the river below.

The sharp cries of the possums in the darkness served as a harsh reminder of where I was and what I needed to do. The echoes of the past, the guilt, and the unresolved questions about Jamie all collided in my mind, creating a maelstrom of emotions. The memory of that fateful afternoon on the bridge in Queensland lingered like a shadow. I had watched my best mate, being swept away by the river's current, a witness to the consequences of my own anger and impulsiveness.

That moment had been defined by my teenage naiveté, a reckless mix of emotion and pride. I remembered the small, crumpled piece of scrap paper that Jamie had dropped as he fell. 'Killerton Enterprises' it had read – two words that had haunted me for years, a cryptic message that had never quite left the periphery of my consciousness.

Now, years later, those words seemed to hold more significance than ever. The night around me felt oppressively silent, the darkness deepening as I tried to reconcile the past with the present. The unsent message on my phone, addressed to Jamie, glowed accusingly in the dark. My finger hovered over the send button, a part of me hesitant, but the rational part of my mind knew better. With a swift movement, I erased the message, the bright light from the screen momentarily blinding me in the pitch-black environment.

I shook my head, trying to clear the fog of memories and emotions. I closed the door of the car, the soft click echoing in the silence. The cold night air seeped into the car, wrapping around me like a chilly embrace. I sat there, enveloped in darkness, staring at Luke's house, which remained as still and silent as ever.

As time ticked by, the night seemed to draw its veil tighter around me, the hours stretching on with an eerie stillness.

My mind raced with thoughts, theories, and possibilities. This investigation was more than just a case; it was a journey into a past that I had never fully left behind. The answers I sought were out there, hidden in the shadows of the night.

4338.210

(29 July 2018)

THE DECISION

4338.210.1

The first rays of dawn brought a soft light over the hillside, gently illuminating the interior of my car. Despite my determination to keep watch on the house, the toll of the long, sleepless night was evident in my struggle to suppress yet another yawn. The sky transitioned from a deep navy to a lighter shade of blue, signalling the end of my vigil. Reluctantly, after an hour more of surveillance, knowing I needed to be sharp for the day ahead at the station, I decided it was time to get even just a couple of hours of sleep.

As I stretched my arms out, trying to ease the stiffness that had settled in my joints, a series of loud cracks echoed in the confined space of the car. In my fatigue, I pushed my hands outward a little too enthusiastically and accidentally struck the steering wheel. The car horn blared out a short, sharp honk, shattering the silence that had enveloped the night. Startled, I jumped, my head colliding with the roof of the car in a comical yet painful encounter.

Instinctively, my first reaction was to check if anyone had witnessed my less-than-graceful moment. My eyes darted across the street, scanning the early morning shadows for any signs of life, any potential onlookers who might have seen my startled jump.

And then, out of the corner of my eye, I saw it. A subtle movement. The blinds in the front lounge on the second floor moved ever so slightly. My heart skipped a beat as a face appeared at the window, peering out. I leaned forward, straining my eyes in an attempt to get a better look, but just as quickly as it appeared, the face withdrew, leaving me with nothing but a fleeting glimpse.

The fleeting glimpse of someone behind the blinds had transformed the entire scenario. The house, once a silent enigma in the night, now held a tangible clue. My weariness evaporated, replaced by a rush of adrenaline and a renewed sense of purpose. Someone was in there – watching, waiting. This could be the breakthrough we needed in the case of Jamie and Kain's disappearance.

As I sat in the car, my heart racing, the light of dawn cast a golden glow over me. I knew I wasn't officially on duty, but the possibility of encountering Luke, Jamie, or Kain was too critical to ignore. I had to act, had to seize this chance to uncover the truth.

With a sense of urgency, I got out of the car and sprinted towards Luke's house. The morning light bathed the neighbourhood in a soft, ethereal quality. I slowed to a walk as I approached the driveway, trying to calm my racing heart and catch my breath.

Reaching the front porch, I climbed the three short steps with a mix of caution and determination. My hand raised to knock sharply on the wooden door, my mind racing with a myriad of excuses for my presence at this early hour. Each justification sounded more absurd than the last. Despite being a police officer, I had no badge, no gun – my usual symbols of authority and safety were conspicuously absent.

"Shit," I muttered under my breath, the gravity of my recklessness hitting me. *What had I been thinking?* I had just impulsively knocked on a door without any idea of what, or who, awaited me on the other side. I was unarmed, without any official identification, essentially just a man standing on a doorstep. The realisation of the potential danger I had put myself in began to dawn on me.

For several long minutes, I stood in front of the door, a bundle of nerves. The door remained steadfastly closed, a silent barrier between me and the answers I sought. Against my better judgment, driven by determination, I knocked again, harder this time. The sound echoed through the quiet morning air, surely loud enough to wake not just the occupants of the house but the neighbours as well. Yet, there was no response, only the sound of my own heart pounding in my ears, a relentless drumbeat of anticipation.

Convinced that I hadn't been mistaken about the movement behind the blinds or the fleeting glimpse of a face, I moved cautiously along the side of the house. Peering through the darkened kitchen window, I could see into the living area. The blinds on the other side of the house, the ones I was sure I had seen the face behind, were closed. The room was empty, bathed in the pale grey light of early dawn. I watched intently, scanning every inch of the visible space for any sign of movement or life. But there was nothing, just the stillness of an uninhabited room.

I couldn't shake the feeling that something was off, that there was more to this house than met the eye. Driven by a need to uncover the truth, I made a quick decision. I quietly climbed over the fence that marked the boundary between the driveway and the backyard, landing with a soft thud on the other side.

Staying low, I moved stealthily along the back of the house, my senses heightened. Every shadow, every sound seemed magnified in the quiet of the morning. I approached the back-bedroom window, stopping just short of it. My heart was racing, adrenaline coursing through my veins. This was it, the moment of truth. What lay beyond this window could be the key to unlocking the mystery of Jamie and Kain's disappearance.

As a police officer, I was trained for situations like this, but without my badge or gun, I was just a man, driven by instinct and a determination to find answers. The risks were clear, but so was the necessity of my actions. I readied myself, preparing to look through the window, to finally see what secrets this house was hiding.

As I stood there with my eyes closed, trying to calm my racing mind, I envisioned myself on a secluded beach. The serene image of waves gently crashing against the rocks and the sound of the wind whistling through swaying trees filled my mind, creating a momentary haven of peace amidst the chaos of the investigation. I could almost feel the ocean spray on my face, the cool mist a stark contrast to the tension that had gripped me. For a brief moment, I was transported away from the shadowy reality of my current situation, lost in the tranquility of this mental escape.

But that tranquility was shattered abruptly.

"Who the hell are you?" The voice, sharp and unexpected, jolted me back to reality. My eyes flew open, and the peaceful beach in my mind evaporated like a mirage. My heart hammered in my chest, a stark reminder that I was far from a quiet beach. I felt my face flush with heat, the embarrassment of being caught off guard mixing with a rush of adrenaline.

I turned slowly, dread mixing with curiosity, to face the source of the voice. It came from the other side of the fence, from where I had trespassed earlier in my search for answers. An elderly face, lined with years of life and experience, stared back at me. The expression was one of suspicion and demand, a silent expectation of an explanation. Those eyes, seasoned by time, seemed to pierce through me, searching for the truth behind my presence.

Caught off-guard by the sudden confrontation, I scrambled to find a plausible explanation. There I was, in the backyard of a house I had no right to be in, facing an elderly neighbour whose suspicious gaze was completely justified. I needed to think fast, to conjure a response that wouldn't escalate the situation.

"I'm Karl Jenkins. Detective Karl Jenkins," I blurted out, hastily pulling my wallet from my pocket. I waved it in front of the man, hoping to convey some semblance of authority. The wallet didn't contain a badge, but it was my best shot at legitimising my presence. If I was lucky, he might just assume he'd seen official identification and not question further. "And who are you?"

"Oh, I'm terribly sorry to have interrupted you," the man replied, seemingly taking my bait. Relief washed over me momentarily. "I'm Terry. I live across the street."

"I'm looking for Luke Smith or Jamie Greyson," I continued, pressing for information while I had the chance. "Have you seen either of them?"

"Not in the last few days," Terry answered.

I rummaged through my wallet, searching for a business card. Finding one, I tried to smooth out the large crease running down its centre before handing it over. Terry scrutinised the card, and I braced myself for his response.

"But," Terry began, piquing my interest, "their friend has been here a lot recently. She's made a few trips here in a small truck."

"A small truck," I echoed, surprised at the new information. "How odd. Do you have any idea what for? Are they moving?"

"Not sure. I don't think so. I think she's been making deliveries of some kind. I've not noticed anything leaving the house," Terry replied.

"Very odd indeed. Well, do call me if you see or hear anything else, sir," I said, nudging the conversation to a close. Terry didn't seem to have any more information, and my patience was wearing thin.

"Of course," Terry said, accepting the role of a makeshift neighbourhood watch. "I'll make sure you're the first person I call."

"Brilliant!" I replied, perhaps a bit too eagerly. An awkward silence hung between us, each of us unsure how to exit the conversation gracefully.

"Well, I'll leave you to it then," Terry finally said, breaking the silence.

"Terry?" I called out just as he began to walk away. A lingering curiosity compelled me to ask one more question. "Have you seen anyone else around here? Last night or this morning?"

"No, sir. Only you," Terry replied with a grin that unsettled me. The way he maintained eye contact was slightly unnerving.

I nodded, watching as Terry slowly made his way back across the street. His grin lingered in my mind, an odd detail in an already peculiar conversation. I stood there for a moment longer, mulling over what Terry had said about the small truck and the deliveries. It was a lead, albeit a strange one. As Terry disappeared into his house, I turned back towards Luke's house, my mind racing with questions and theories. *Who was this friend with the truck? What were they delivering? And most importantly, how did it all connect to Jamie and Kain's disappearance?*

Regaining my composure after the unsettling interaction with Terry, I turned my attention back to Luke's house. Peering through the gap in the almost closed blinds of the back-bedroom window, I scrutinised the scene inside. The gap appeared unchanged from my previous observation. The mystery of who I had seen in the front blinds lingered in my mind, an unanswered question that added to the complexity of the situation. There was no sign of anyone now, the room appearing empty and still.

But something felt off. My instincts, honed from years on the force, were ringing alarm bells. I focused on the black garbage bags I had noticed earlier. They were still there, piled up in the room. However, something was different this time. I began to count them quietly, a growing sense of unease accompanying each number.

"Seven," I whispered to myself, a chill running down my spine. "Shit." My memory was clear – there had been fewer bags when I first saw them yesterday afternoon. This was a clear indication that someone had been in the house since then. If anyone was still inside, they were doing an exceptional job of remaining hidden and silent.

I felt a strong urge to go inside and investigate further, but I was acutely aware of the limitations of my current position. I wasn't on duty, and even if I were, the presence of additional garbage bags wouldn't be sufficient grounds to enter the house without a search warrant. And obtaining a warrant based on this observation alone was a long shot.

Throughout my career, I had encountered many seemingly innocuous scenes that hid darker realities. I had learned not to underestimate the chaos and cruelty that could lurk beneath the surface of wealth and privilege. A clean-looking house in a middle-class suburb could conceal secrets just as well as any rundown hideout. It was a lesson that had stuck with me, a reminder that appearances could be deceiving, and that the truth often required digging deeper than the surface.

Resolved to my decision, I stood there, fully aware of the legal boundaries I was skirting. Breaking and entering was not just a crime – for someone in my profession, it could be a career-ending move. But the temptation, the need for answers was overwhelming.

If I was caught.

Despite my better judgment, curiosity and a detective's instinct took over. I reached out tentatively to the fly screen covering the back-bedroom window. My fingers traced the edges, searching for a vulnerability, a way in that wouldn't leave a trace. A small victory surged through me as I found a weak spot.

"Aha!" The exclamation slipped out louder than I had intended. *I've found it.*

But then, my leg vibrated, startling me. The fly screen clattered to the ground as I fumbled to retrieve my ringing phone. It was Sarah. In that instant, the reality of my actions hit me. I declined the call, my mind a whirlwind of conflicting thoughts.

Regret started to seep in as I tried to replace the screen, an act now feeling more like a cover-up than an investigation. The screen slipped from my grasp again, crashing to the ground. My actions were becoming less like those of a detective and more like those of a desperate man acting on impulse.

As I picked up the screen once more, a dangerous rationale took hold. If Luke was innocent, he would report a break-in, giving us legitimate grounds to enter and investigate. It was a risky gambit, one that straddled the line of legal and ethical conduct.

With one last look around to ensure I wasn't being watched, I made my choice. I rammed my elbow into the window, shattering the glass with a resounding crash. The deed was done – it certainly looked like a break-in.

A sense of satisfaction mixed with guilt painted my expression as I left the property. The gravity of what I had just done weighed heavily on me as I returned to my car and drove home. The silence in the car was deafening, a stark contrast to the chaos of thoughts and emotions swirling inside me.

I had crossed a line, driven by a desire to uncover the truth, but at what cost? The lines between right and wrong, ethical and unethical, had suddenly blurred.

THE TRIFFETT'S

4338.210.2

As I trudged towards the police station, my mind still whirled from the events of the morning. The display on the car dashboard had confirmed my fears – I was late for work, again. The thought of a 'quiet chat' with the Sergeant over my tardiness and the potential blemish on my newly acquired promotion rankled me. I needed to be more cautious.

Opting for the front entrance rather than sneaking in through the back, I hoped my fresh set of clothes would dispel any suspicion that I was just arriving. I strode through the automatic doors and down the ramp leading to the secured door near the reception desk, trying to exude a sense of normalcy and routine.

"I don't understand," I overheard a woman's voice, strained with frustration and worry. She was standing at the reception desk, her back to me.

Pausing before swiping my security card, I couldn't help but eavesdrop on the conversation.

"I haven't seen or heard from my husband since yesterday. How can that not qualify for me to make a missing persons report?" the woman demanded.

I listened intently for the receptionist's reply.

The receptionist's response was matter-of-fact, yet devoid of empathy. "I'm sorry, Mrs Triffett, but you said you received a text message from him last night. That counts as a form of direct contact. Jenny, your husband just isn't missing."

Jenny's distress was palpable as she began to tear up. "But that just isn't like my husband! He would never just leave like that, especially without saying goodbye to little Sammy. And the dog has gone missing too!"

My detective instincts kicked in. *Another disappearance?* The tension in the air was almost tangible. Jenny's desperation, her plea for help, resonated with me, adding another layer of urgency to the already complex web of cases I was entangled in.

"Jenny, you know there's nothing I can do for you. The system doesn't have the resources—" the receptionist tried to say before being cut off abruptly.

"Screw the system!" Jenny's voice broke through my thoughts as she slammed her fist on the countertop. "You know me, Linda. You know my husband! Hell, you had dinner with us just last week. You know Nial would never do this to us!"

The raw emotion in Jenny's voice struck a chord. Her situation, so painfully human, reminded me of the very reason I had chosen this profession. It wasn't just about solving puzzles; it was about helping people in their darkest hours, about bringing answers to those plagued by uncertainty.

"Mrs. Triffett, was it?" I approached her with a gentle tone, trying to offer some semblance of comfort amidst her turmoil.

"Yes," she responded, her voice tinged with confusion as she looked up at me. "Do I know you?"

I felt an unexpected wave of emotion, a reaction to the palpable pain in her bright blue eyes. There was something vaguely familiar about her, a feeling I couldn't quite pin down. "No, I'm Detective Karl Jenkins. Why don't you come with me and you can tell me what's going on."

She hesitated, clearly weighing her trust in a stranger against her desperate need for help. Observing her, I took in her slender, petite frame, the way her golden hair curled around her shoulders, and her two-toned pink-and-black glasses that added a unique touch to her appearance. Her rosy cheeks and pink lips added to her distinct look.

As I swiped my security card and the green light flashed, indicating access, I held the door open for her. "After you, ma'am," I said, maintaining a polite and professional demeanour.

We navigated the maze of corridors until we reached the open interview room at the end of the final narrow corridor. Standing at the entrance, memories of my recent conversation with Louise Jeffries in this very room came flooding back. The thought of another disappearance, another person lost, weighed heavily on me.

"This way please, Mrs. Triffett," I gently guided her into the room. "Please, take a seat."

As she settled into one of the metal-framed chairs, I took a moment to compose myself. The room, stark and functional, seemed to amplify the gravity of our conversation. Each disappearance case was a stark reminder of the unpredictability of life and the fragility of human connections. As a detective, it was my duty to piece together these fragmented lives, to bring clarity and resolution to those left in the wake of uncertainty. With a deep breath, I prepared to listen to Mrs. Triffett's story, ready to delve into another mystery, another human story needing to be understood and resolved.

Waiting for her to get comfortable, I pulled up the second chair and faced her directly. Retrieving a small pad and pen from my shirt pocket, I prepared to jot down the details of her story. "Your full name, please?" I asked, pen poised above the paper.

"Jenny Triffett," she replied succinctly.

"Thank you," I responded, carefully writing her name in capital letters at the top of the notepad. I added the date in the top right corner: *Sunday, 29 July 2018.*

Lifting my gaze back to Jenny, I was momentarily struck by her beauty. It was rare for me to find myself at a loss for words, but her presence momentarily disarmed me. My mouth moved as if to speak, yet no sound came out.

Not waiting for me to regain my composure, Jenny took the initiative. "My husband, Nial, is missing. He has been since yesterday morning," she said, her voice laced with a mix of determination and underlying worry.

Regaining my professional focus, I asked, "How do you know he has gone missing?"

"Because I haven't seen him since yesterday morning," she responded with a bluntness that matched my own.

"But you have heard from him, yeah? That is what the receptionist was saying, right?" I inquired, recalling the conversation I had overheard at the reception desk.

"I thought Linda was my friend," said Jenny coldly, looking away from me.

"Linda?" I asked, not sure who she was referring to.

Jenny turned back to face me. "Linda. The receptionist," she said, her tone growing impatient with the conversation.

"So, you know her then," I stated.

"Yes. Apart from also being my sister-in-law, our families have known each other for years. We share great grandmothers on my mother's side," Jenny explained.

Her response drew a chuckle from me. "You must be Tasmanian, then," I commented, trying to lighten the mood with a touch of local humour. I noticed a subtle change in Jenny's demeanour as she seemed to relax slightly.

"Yes. A bit obvious that, isn't it?" she responded with a small laugh. Her subsequent question about my origins caught me off guard. "Are you from here?"

I smiled, appreciating the brief respite from the heaviness of our conversation. "No," I replied. "I was born in South

Australia, but my family moved to Queensland when I was a young boy. Somehow, I've ended up here."

Jenny's smile in response was a brief moment of solace amidst the storm of her current situation. Despite the anxiety and frustration she was clearly feeling, there was an undeniable warmth about her. It made me ponder the nature of her husband's disappearance. *How could someone just leave a woman like her?* The thought lingered in my mind as I redirected my focus back to the investigation at hand.

"Tell me about the last time you saw your husband," I said.

Jenny took a deep breath, then explained. "Nial had just finished in the shower. He was staring off into the mirror. He was distracted. I could tell something was bothering him, so I rubbed his damp shoulder gently. It always relaxed him so quickly when I did that."

I bet it did, I thought to myself. I wanted to interrupt and ask if she knew what was bothering her husband, but I was too distracted by the soft, eloquent, beautiful way her words floated out of her mouth, and I shifted uncomfortably in my chair instead.

"And then his phone rang. He went off to the bedroom to take the call," she continued, adding another layer to the narrative.

My eyes closed briefly. My hand rubbed at my brow, bringing back my focus. "Do you know who he was speaking to?" I asked, curious about the nature of the call that seemed to have preceded his departure.

"No. I disrobed myself and got into the shower," Jenny replied, maintaining her composure despite the personal nature of the details.

I shifted in my chair, trying to maintain professionalism despite the intimate details being shared. "What happened after the phone call?" I pressed, eager to piece together the timeline of events.

"Well, I was still in the shower when he poked his head in to say that he was just going out to meet with a new client about a potential fencing job. And then I assume he left," she recounted.

"You assume?" I echoed, wanting to clarify her last statement.

"When I was done in the shower, he was not about. His ute was also gone," she explained, confirming that Nial had left the house without a direct farewell.

This new information about a potential job and Nial leaving without a proper goodbye was intriguing. It suggested a sudden or unplanned departure, or perhaps a deeper issue that Jenny might not be aware of. I noted down every detail, aware that even the smallest piece of information could be crucial.

"And the dog? Did you say before that your dog was also missing?"

"Yes," Jenny began, "And no," she quickly corrected herself, causing me to look up in confusion.

"Well, yes, Buffy is now missing. But she wasn't earlier in the morning. Sammy was playing with her after Nial had left." Her clarification painted a picture of a normal morning that had suddenly turned abnormal.

"Sammy, your son?" I confirmed, wanting to make sure I understood the family dynamics correctly.

"Yes. He's three." Jenny's voice trembled as she spoke about her son. "He misses his father so much already. He was so upset when Nial wasn't there to tuck him into bed and read him his bedtime story. They have a nightly routine," she said, tears welling up in her eyes.

I reached out instinctively, offering a comforting touch to her shaking hands. "It's okay, Jenny. We'll find Nial," I reassured her, though I was well aware of the unpredictable nature of these cases.

Her next words caught me off guard. "Why aren't all police officers as kind as you?" she asked, a hint of bitterness in her voice.

I was puzzled. "What do you mean? Have you already spoken to another officer?" I inquired, sensing there was more to her story.

"Yes, of course," she replied quickly, confirming my suspicion.

"Really? Please, do tell," I urged her, eager to understand the full context.

"Well naturally, after Buffy disappeared, which gave me quite the fright, I called the police to report her disappearance," she began, pausing for a moment. "And Nial's," she added.

"But they didn't seem too worried about Nial, did they, Mrs Triffett?" I asked carefully.

"No," Jenny replied with a huff.

"And why was that?" I urged her to continue, gently trying to coax out the details.

Jenny's pause, her eyes closing as she gathered her thoughts, spoke volumes. I could sense her internal struggle, the battle between wanting to share the truth and fear of judgment. "You can tell me the truth, Jenny. I won't judge you," I assured her, hoping to provide a sense of safety and understanding.

"Judge me! You're no different to the rest of them. I know what you're all thinking," she retorted, her frustration and hurt palpable.

I didn't need her to elaborate; I understood the implication. "They questioned his fidelity, didn't they?" I asked, though I already knew the answer.

"Yes," she confirmed quietly, her voice barely above a whisper.

I pressed on, knowing there was more to the story. "And there was something else you told them, wasn't there, Jenny? Something that pressed them to conclude that you had no case for a missing person's report."

Her affirmative response was a mere whisper, accompanied by a single tear that betrayed the emotional toll this ordeal was taking on her. I felt a lump in my throat, empathising with her pain, and softly asked, "What did you tell them?"

"While the police were with me, I received a text message from Nial. He said that he was still with the potential client and was going to be home late," she revealed, her eyes still closed.

"Fuck!" The expletive slipped out before I could stop it, reflecting the complexity and the frustration of the situation. A text message from Nial could significantly alter the nature of the case, yet it also deepened the mystery. *Why hadn't he come home as he said he would? Was there more to his disappearance than met the eye?*

Jenny's gaze, deep and blue, held a raw intensity that seemed to reach right into me. As I instinctively leaned back, the chair's metal legs scraped against the hard floor, a jarring sound in the otherwise silent room. Before I could muster an apology, another tear traced its way down Jenny's cheek, deepening my sense of helplessness in the face of her sorrow.

"He told me not to wait up for him," Jenny continued, her voice laden with a mixture of confusion and hurt. "He's never said that to me before." Her words hung in the air, heavy with implication.

I found myself at a crossroads, uncertain whether to offer comfort or to maintain a professional distance. Her account, while poignant, did seem to lean more towards the possibility of infidelity than a straightforward missing person's case. The implications were unsettling.

A wave of concern washed over me, the hairs on my arms standing on end. The lack of direct contact, the hint of strain in their relationship—it all felt too coincidental, too aligned with the patterns of troubled partnerships I had heard about in recent days.

"Do you know of a Luke Smith?" I ventured, probing for any potential connection that might shed light on the situation.

Jenny pondered for a moment, and in that pause, the tension in the room seemed to amplify. "No. The name doesn't sound familiar. Should I know him?" she inquired, her confusion evident.

"No," I replied, choosing not to delve deeper into that line of questioning. It was clear that mentioning Luke Smith would only lead her down a path of further distress without any substantial reason.

Jenny's next plea was heartfelt. "Are you going to help me?"

I couldn't refuse. I reached for another business card and slid it across the table to her. "I'll open a case file," I promised. "I need you to contact me the moment you hear anything further from your husband. Anything at all," I emphasised, wanting her to understand the importance of any new information.

"Of course," she responded, her hand briefly touching mine in gratitude. The contact sent an unexpected shiver through me, a reminder of the human connection at the heart of this case. "Whatever you need to do your job."

I managed a smile, though it felt awkward under the weight of the situation. Jenny's plight had become more than just another case to me. Her pain, her uncertainty, resonated deeply, and I was committed to uncovering the truth, no matter where it might lead. As she held my business card, I saw in her eyes a glimmer of hope, a hope that I was determined not to let fade.

❖

"Who was that?" Sarah asked as I walked back into the open-plan office, pen in hand and notebook still open to the notes I had made from Jenny's interview. Sarah never did seem to miss much when it came to my movements.

"Jenny Triffett," I responded, offering only the name as I clutched my pen and notebook, the pages still open to my freshly written notes from the interview. I had no intention of divulging more details, especially since I was already planning to hand over the notes to Glen. My workload was heavy, dominated by the ongoing cases involving Jamie and Luke.

"Who's Jenny Triffett?" Sarah probed further, her curiosity piqued.

"The wife of Nial Triffett, of course," I replied, barely suppressing a smile. Sarah's assumption that I was intentionally keeping her in the dark amused me. I toyed with the idea of prolonging her curiosity a bit longer.

Her response was immediate and physical—a firm thump on my shoulder. I quickly reconsidered my playful stance.

"We need to advise the officers to be on the lookout for Nial Triffett's work ute," I stated, shifting the focus back to the case. It was essential to act quickly, regardless of who was officially assigned to the case. Finding Nial's ute could be crucial to resolving the case swiftly. Besides, I couldn't help but feel a bit curious about the developments myself.

"Why? What's up? Something else related to the investigation?" Sarah's enthusiasm was evident, always eager to delve into the details of a case.

"I'm not sure yet," I admitted. "His wife said he went to visit a potential new client for his struggling fencing business yesterday and has now gone missing. But—" I began to explain, but before I could continue, Sarah cut me off.

"Well, that definitely sounds like it could be connected," she said, jumping to unnecessary conclusions again. "Do we know who he went to visit?" she asked.

"No," I said, frowning. "And Jenny called the police last night. While they were there talking to her, she received a text message from Nial telling her that he would be late home and not to wait up for him," I explained.

Sarah frowned back at me. "That does sound a lot more like a case of infidelity than a missing person, and last time I checked, being a slimy cheat wasn't actually against the law," she said, clearly disappointed that it wasn't another lead for our investigation.

"You're right," I conceded, "but I think it's worth digging a bit deeper." My instincts as a detective told me not to dismiss any possibilities too soon. "I'm sure Glen won't mind us helping out a bit," I added, more to myself than Sarah, as I took a seat at my desk.

"Glen has the case?" she asked. "God help that poor woman."

Chuckling, I opened up the car registration database and began typing in the details of Nial's ute. The search yielded a result almost immediately. Scribbling the number plate on a yellow Post-it note, I handed it to Sarah. "Here, go put out a BOLO for Nial's ute, would you?" I requested.

Sarah read the number plate aloud, double-checking the hastily written characters. "Tasmania's a small place. I can't imagine his ute staying hidden for long," she observed, walking to her desk to put out the Be On the LookOut (BOLO) alert.

Leaning back in my chair, the puzzle pieces of the Triffett case swirled in my mind. The complexity of the situation was like a knot, each element intertwining with the others – the enigmatic text from Nial, Jenny's distress, and the peculiar detail of the missing dog.

"Oh, Sarah. I almost forgot," I called out, remembering a crucial step in our investigation. "Make a note to get a copy of Nial's phone records. Let's see if we can find out who he may have gone to visit." Such details could provide vital clues.

"On it," Sarah replied promptly.

While Sarah worked on that, I turned to my computer, drawn to an old, nagging mystery that had haunted me for years: Killerton Enterprises. Typing the name into the search engine brought up the familiar result – the American construction company that seemed entirely unrelated to the mysterious note Jamie had left years ago. The disparity between the note and the results of my search was frustrating. This American company, now worth over a billion dollars, had no apparent connection to Australia. Yet, that name had clearly frightened young Jamie all those years ago.

I stared at the screen, lost in thought. The Killerton Enterprises I was looking for seemed to be a phantom, existing nowhere but in Jamie's past and potentially my ongoing investigation. It was a dead end that I had hit time and again, but something in me refused to let it go. There had to be a connection, a reason why that name had been significant enough for Jamie to scribble it down on a piece of scrap paper.

Sarah's voice cut through my thoughts. Hastily, I closed the browser window. The last thing I needed was for Sarah to stumble upon my private investigation into Killerton Enterprises, especially considering how I had lost Jamie's scrap paper after transferring to the Tasmanian Police. It was a secret I intended to keep.

"Found something already?" I inquired as Sarah approached my desk.

"Yes," she replied, but her quick clarification that it wasn't about the Triffetts caught my attention. "It's about Jamie and Kain," she added.

I couldn't hide my irritation. "Shit, Sarah," I said, frustrated. Information on Jamie's case was too critical to be delayed, especially given my personal connection and the recent reckless actions I had taken.

Sarah updated me on her findings. "I've spoken with both the Launceston and Hobart airports. There's no record of either Jamie or Kain having boarded a plane in the last two weeks."

"Which means they have to still be in the state," I said eagerly. "At least that keeps our searching area fairly narrow." My mind was already racing with the implications of this new information, but then a thought struck me. "What about the Spirit of Tasmania? Have you checked with them yet?"

Sarah took a deep breath before responding. "Yes. I've spoken with the Spirit too. They have no records of Jamie or Kain having boarded in the last two weeks either. But Duncan is bringing down a copy of their security footage. They could have used aliases. And there is always the slim chance that they snuck on board."

"Very slim chance," I agreed, nodding. "But very good work Sarah. That's going to keep you busy for a while." Her thoroughness was commendable. The prospect of going through security footage was daunting, yet necessary.

THE DRIVER

4338.210.3

"There! Look!" Sarah exclaimed, her finger jabbing excitedly towards a car that had just screeched around a corner, emerging from the bottle shop's car park. Its abrupt turn sent a flock of pigeons into a frenzied flight, their wings fluttering in alarm.

"Shit! That was a close call," I breathed out, my eyes tracking the driver's reckless manoeuvre. The car, a silver Honda Civic, swerved perilously close to a small red hatchback, its parked position on the roadside making it an innocent bystander in this near-miss. My heart pounded in my chest, a mix of adrenaline and professional alertness surging through me.

"Random?" asked Sarah, her eyebrows raised inquisitively.

"It would be irresponsible of us not to," I agreed, feeling a wide grin stretch across my face. Our involvement in pulling over cars for random breath tests wasn't a frequent occurrence, but sometimes the situation just screamed for it. A sense of satisfaction bubbled within me at the thought of catching someone in the act. Why people gambled with the lives of others, thinking they could slip away unnoticed, especially after blatantly pulling out of a bottle shop, was beyond me.

Sarah's grin mirrored my own, a sparkle of mischief in her eyes. "Here we go then," she said, her voice tinged with an eagerness that was almost gleeful. She flicked on the red and blue flashing lights, their glow painting the interior of our unmarked police car in a dance of colours. The siren blared briefly, a clear signal to the Honda Civic that its actions hadn't gone unnoticed.

Following the Civic, I steered our car with practiced ease, pulling up behind it as the driver finally acknowledged our presence, easing to a stop along the main road threading through Glenorchy.

"You want to do the honours?" I asked, turning to Sarah with a knowing look.

"Sure," she replied, her eagerness palpable. She was always ready to jump into action.

"I'll do a plate check," I added, watching as Sarah stepped out of our car. Her movements were confident, each step calculated as she approached the other vehicle.

Purposely delaying the start of the license plate check, I found myself watching Sarah. Her approach to the driver's side was assertive yet measured. Leaning forward, she began to speak to the driver, her posture professional but unmistakably commanding.

After watching Sarah instruct the drunk driver to blow into the pen-sized plastic tube, a standard but crucial procedure, I shifted my focus to the more mundane task at hand. Sitting in our unmarked police car, I began to enter the vehicle's number plate details into the database. I tapped the keys with practiced efficiency, my mind half on the task, half on Sarah's interaction outside. The screen before me flickered with the irritating "processing" message, a pixelated hourglass spinning endlessly as it sifted through thousands of vehicle records. My patience, usually unwavering, was tested by the sluggish system.

Finally, the database emitted a beep, a sound signalling successful retrieval. My eyes narrowed in concentration as I scanned the information displayed. A name flickered on the screen, causing my eyebrows to furrow in confusion. "Surely that's not right," I muttered under my breath, disbelief colouring my tone.

Before I could fully process the anomaly or step out to verify, Sarah returned, her expression a mix of professionalism and evident disappointment. I wound down the window to speak with her.

"Well, that's a bit disappointing. She's recorded a zero blood-alcohol reading," Sarah announced, her voice laced with a hint of frustration.

"She?" I echoed, my confusion deepening. The name on the screen didn't match the situation unfolding.

"Yeah," Sarah confirmed, extending the driver's license towards me. The plastic card felt cool and firm in my hand as I examined it. *Gladys Cramer,*' the name stared back at me, incongruent with my expectations. "I think we might have a little problem," I murmured, more to myself than to Sarah.

"What is it?" Sarah inquired, her curiosity piqued.

"Is Gladys the only person in the car?" I asked, seeking confirmation of a growing suspicion.

"Yeah. Why?" Her response was quick, yet I sensed her growing unease.

"This car belongs to Jamie Greyson." The name rolled off my tongue, heavy with implications.

"Shit!" Sarah exclaimed, the gravity of the situation dawning on her. "Ok, what do you want me to do?" she asked, as her hand instinctively moved towards her holster. "Should I get my gun out?"

"No! Jesus, Sarah, what is it with you and your bloody gun?" I snapped, my tone sharper than intended. Sarah's readiness to escalate to force was a recurring point of contention between us. "You wait here. I'll deal with her," I said, determination settling over me like armour.

Easing myself out of the car, I felt the cool air brush against my skin. My mind was already working overtime, piecing together the puzzle. *Who was Gladys Cramer, and why was she driving Jamie Greyson's car?* As I closed the door behind me, my steps were measured, my mind racing with possibilities.

My footsteps echoing slightly on the asphalt as I approached the silver Honda Civic. I could feel the weight of my badge, a constant reminder of the responsibility I carried. Stopping beside the driver's side window, I peered inside, meeting the eyes of the woman behind the wheel.

"Gladys Cramer?" I asked sternly, extending the license towards her. My tone was authoritative, yet not unkind, a balance I had learned to strike over years of police work.

"Yes," the woman replied, her voice laced with a casual curiosity. "Have I done something wrong?" she inquired, her tone betraying nothing but innocent inquiry.

"I'm Senior Detective Karl Jenkins," I introduced myself formally, maintaining a professional demeanour. "Is this your car, ma'am?" I continued, scrutinising her every reaction.

Gladys hesitated for just a fraction of a second before answering. "No," she admitted. "It's a friend's car. He told me I could use it to go to the bottle shop," she explained, gesturing towards a bulging brown paper bag on the passenger seat. The bag, evidently heavy with bottles, leaned against the seat as if to corroborate her story. "We were planning on having a trashy movie binge session, but then we realised we didn't have any drinks to go with it. He's at home cooking now, which is why I went to get the wine," she added, her explanation flowing smoothly.

I paused, taking a moment to process the information. My mind sifted through her words, analysing their credibility. "Who is this friend of yours?" I asked, my curiosity piqued.

"Oh, Jamie Greyson, of course. This is his car," she responded matter-of-factly, as if mentioning an everyday acquaintance.

"Jamie Greyson, did you say?" I repeated, a flicker of surprise crossing my features. A kaleidoscope of butterflies erupted in my stomach, the sudden rush of adrenaline surprising even me. *Is this whole investigation about to end so anti-climatically?* The thought crossed my mind, mingling with a mix of skepticism and hope.

"Yes," Gladys confirmed, her response simple yet loaded with implications.

"Well, how's that for timing," I remarked, a surge of energy coursing through my words. "We've been trying to contact Jamie for the last few days. We'll just follow you back to his house, if you don't mind," I said, carefully masking the excitement that was building within me. My gaze never left her face, watching for any telltale signs of deceit.

Gladys glanced nervously towards the passenger seat, her eyes betraying a momentary flicker of uncertainty. "Not at all," she replied, her smile forced but strikingly beautiful.

"Alright then," I said, tapping the edge of her car as a sign of departure. I turned and walked back to our vehicle, my mind racing with possibilities. *Was Gladys telling the truth? Was this encounter with Jamie Greyson's car merely a red-herring, or are there really no missing people?* I couldn't shake the feeling that we were on the cusp of unraveling something significant.

❖

"Well?" Sarah queried impatiently, her eyes eager for the details as I slid back into the driver's seat.

I secured my seatbelt. "Well," I began, unable to suppress a grin at Sarah's eagerness. "It seems we are about to find Jamie Greyson."

Sarah rolled her eyes, a playful but exasperated gesture. "Well, where's the fun in that!?" she lamented, her tone half-joking yet revealing a hint of genuine disappointment.

I turned the key, the engine of our car purring to life. "Not everything has to end with murder and crime," I reminded her, my tone laced with a mix of amusement and seriousness.

"I know, I know," Sarah grumbled, her frustration evident. "But I haven't investigated a murder yet. I thought maybe this might be my first." Her words echoed a longing for the kind of action that had probably drawn her to detective work in the first place.

"Well, looks like you're about to be disappointed... Officer," I replied, emphasising the last word to underline the professional restraint we were expected to uphold, regardless of our personal feelings towards a case.

We fell into silence as we began tailing Gladys's car. The journey took us up the steep and winding Berriedale Road. I kept my eyes fixed on the road ahead, every sense attuned to the task at hand, while Sarah observed Gladys's movements with the intensity of a seasoned officer.

"You've got to be kidding me!" Sarah exclaimed suddenly. "Does it look like Gladys is texting to you?" Her training in spotting distracted drivers was evident; she could identify such behaviour with almost uncanny accuracy.

I squinted through the windshield, trying to get a better look. "Yeah. It sure looks that way, doesn't it?" The dark presence of a phone screen was intermittently visible in the distance.

"Lights or just keep following?" Sarah asked, ready to spring into action.

I was weighing the options when suddenly Gladys' car swerved sharply to the left, nearly grazing the metal barrier that bordered the road. "Shit! We'd better pull her over," I decided without hesitation, recognising the immediate danger.

Sarah didn't hesitate, activating the red and blue flashing lights. But to our surprise, Gladys didn't respond immediately. She continued driving erratically, her car swerving as she seemed engrossed in her phone. Sarah sounded the siren, a clear command for compliance. Finally, Gladys seemed to acknowledge our presence, pulling over to the side of the road.

I brought our car to a halt behind hers, my mind racing with questions and concerns. *What was so important that Gladys risked her safety and that of others by texting while driving?*

As I stepped out of our vehicle, I glanced back at Sarah, who was already on the move, her hand on the door handle, ready to join me. "You wait in the driver's seat," I instructed firmly. I could see the protest forming in her eyes, the hunger for action almost palpable.

"Just in case she decides to do a runner," I added, knowing full well that the possibility would pique Sarah's interest. Her expression shifted from frustration to anticipation, her eyes gleaming at the thought of a potential pursuit. I couldn't help but shake my head slightly as I turned away, torn between concern over Gladys' possible flight and the eagerness I saw in Sarah for a chase.

Approaching Gladys's car, I heard the mechanical sound of the driver's side window lowering. "Gladys," I began, my voice carrying a tone of disappointment, "why were you texting while you were driving?"

"I wasn't texting," Gladys responded quickly, her voice firm.

"But you were," I countered, unyielding. "My partner and I saw you. We watched you almost run off the road. You could have done yourself some serious harm, or worse, gone over the embankment." My words were stern, but there was an undercurrent of genuine concern for her safety.

"I already told you. I wasn't texting anyone," Gladys repeated, her voice laced with adamant denial.

A sense of frustration began to simmer within me. It was clear that she was hiding something, or someone. My thoughts raced - *she has to be protecting someone. Who is it? Jamie? Kain?* The pieces weren't quite fitting together.

"Gladys," I said, my tone more stern now, "Who were you texting?" I fixed her with a steady gaze, trying to penetrate the façade she was putting up.

Under my scrutiny, I noticed Gladys's discomfort intensify. Her left eye twitched slightly, a subtle tell that she was under stress. She seemed to be struggling to maintain eye contact, her gaze darting around as if seeking an escape.

"I told you. I didn't text anybody. Here, check my phone for yourself," she blurted out, a mix of defiance and desperation in her voice. She unlocked her phone with a hurried swipe and thrust it into my hands.

Holding Gladys's phone, I felt the residual warmth from her hands, a subtle reminder of the human element always present in police work. As I gazed at the unlocked screen, I was acutely aware that what I was about to do could reveal much about her recent actions.

I was treading a fine line, a delicate balance between investigation and privacy. But in handing over the phone voluntarily, Gladys had implicitly given me permission. This small act had legally opened the door for me to delve deeper. *She has verbally given me permission to look through it*, I reassured myself, justifying the action as I navigated to her messages. The name Beatrix Cramer at the top of the message list caught my eye, igniting recognition.

How could I have missed it? Gladys Cramer and Beatrix Cramer - sisters. The realisation hit me with a mix of surprise and a tinge of embarrassment. Beatrix, a figure from a case years ago, one who had left a lasting impression. And Gladys, her sister, whom I had met but only in passing. The memories were hazy, like looking through frosted glass. I recalled Gladys' long, black hair, contrasting with her appearance now. The years had changed her, adding a few extra kilos to her frame, not much but enough to alter her from the vague image I retained in my memory.

Forcing my attention back to the task at hand, I refocused on Gladys's phone. The past connections were intriguing, but they wouldn't solve the case at hand. As I scrolled through the contacts in her message history, I found Jamie's name. Surprisingly, it wasn't as recent as I had anticipated. "I see you haven't messaged Jamie since yesterday," I commented aloud, eyes scanning the last message she had sent him:

Gladys: *Sorry to hear you don't feel well. Call me when you wake up. G.*

This message painted a picture of concern, but it raised more questions than it answered. "Did he call you?" I asked, my tone edged with suspicion. I was playing for time, trying to piece together the fragments of information into a coherent narrative.

While Gladys was responding, I quickly navigated to the call history. The last call logged was to Luke Smith, a mere thirteen seconds long, and it had been placed only minutes ago.

"Of course he did," Gladys retorted sharply, her impatience showing as she snatched her phone back. "I'm on my way to his house in his car, aren't I?" Her response was snappy, her tone defensive. It was clear she was feeling pressured, perhaps even cornered.

I mentally noted her reaction. The exchange had given me just enough time to see what I needed without revealing my discovery of the call to Luke Smith. Gladys's defensiveness, coupled with the brief call to Luke, sent my detective instincts into overdrive. My gut was telling me that Luke Smith was definitely up to no good.

"Our mistake then," I conceded, adopting a tone of polite professionalism. It was important to maintain a facade of routine procedure, at least until I could delve deeper into Luke Smith's involvement. "Shall we continue?" I suggested, gesturing up the road towards Jamie and Luke's house. The suggestion was tactical, a move to keep Gladys cooperative and under observation.

Gladys nodded, a silent agreement to my proposal.

My stride back to the car was quick and purposeful, a clear reflection of the urgency and intensity of the situation. I could feel the adrenaline coursing through my veins, fuelling my movements. Jumping into the passenger side, I barely managed to contain the urge to rush. Every second felt crucial, and I was keenly aware of the importance of what we were about to uncover.

"Did you give her a ticket?" Sarah's question came almost immediately as I settled into the seat.

"No, just drive," I responded, my voice firm and focused. There was no time to explain the complexities of what I had just discovered, and issuing a ticket was the least of our concerns at the moment.

Sarah, sensing the gravity in my tone, asked no more questions. She put the car into gear and followed Gladys's vehicle. The tension in the car was palpable as we drove towards our destination, each of us lost in our thoughts about the case.

THE VOICE

4338.210.4

Parking across the road, we watched as Gladys pulled into Luke Smith's driveway. I noticed Sarah's hesitation to get out of the car, a familiar pause that I had seen many times before. It was the hesitation of an officer brimming with questions, eager for answers yet uncertain of the next step.

"I don't think we're going to be meeting Jamie Greyson," I told her, aiming to address the first question I knew was on her mind.

Sarah turned to me, her expression a mix of confusion and curiosity. "Huh?" she uttered, the single syllable heavy with unspoken queries.

"But with a bit of luck, we might be about to speak with Luke Smith," I continued, allowing a small grin to play on my lips. "He's cooking for her." The revelation was significant, potentially a turning point in our investigation, and I could see the realisation dawning on Sarah's face.

Her eyes widened, a spark of excitement and understanding illuminating her features. It was a look I had come to know well - the thrill of a new lead, the anticipation of uncovering the truth.

"Come on," I said with a smile, encouraging her out of the car. My tone was light, but underneath lay a current of determination. This was a critical moment in our investigation, and I felt a keen sense of responsibility to see it through.

❖

As Sarah and I approached the house, the scene was already unfolding before us. Gladys stood at the front door, her repeated knocks echoing into the silence of the afternoon. She turned to us as we stepped onto the porch. "Well, that's a bit odd," she commented calmly. "There doesn't seem to be anybody home. I wasn't gone that long."

Sarah, always eager for action, couldn't hide her disappointment, letting out a loud, frustrated huff. It was clear she had been hoping for a more immediate confrontation, a resolution to the investigation's mysteries.

My eyes drifted to the set of keys in Gladys' hand, the metal glinting in the sunlight. "But you have a key, don't you, Gladys?" I asked pointedly, focusing on the keys that included those to Jamie's car.

Gladys' response was a nervous laugh, a clear sign of her growing discomfort. "Oh, yeah," she said, lifting the keys with a jingle, trying to brush off her oversight as a mere forgetfulness. "How silly of me."

I continued to observe her, letting the silence hang for a moment. "Well, aren't you going to invite us in?" I asked, my voice calm but firm. I wanted to maintain a professional yet subtly pressing demeanour.

"Wouldn't it be a bit rude of us to enter Jamie's house if he wasn't home?" Gladys retorted, her eyes meeting mine with a hint of anxious desperation. It was clear she was trying to dissuade us, to keep us from uncovering whatever might be waiting inside.

I smiled softly, a gesture meant to reassure yet convey my determination. "I'm pretty sure he wouldn't have given you his keys if he didn't want you being here," I countered, gently undermining her argument.

Sarah, unable to contain herself, let out a short, quiet snort, quickly covering her mouth in a bid for composure.

Her reaction, though unprofessional, was a testament to the tension we all felt.

Gladys' glare shifted from Sarah back to me, her expression a mixture of resignation and reluctance. "I guess so," she conceded with a slight shrug, the movement betraying her inner turmoil.

As she slid the key into the lock, I felt my heart rate accelerate, anticipation coursing through me. Holding my breath, I watched intently as the key turned slowly, the sound of the lock disengaging loud in the quiet of the afternoon. A rush of adrenaline surged through me as the door unlocked with a definitive click.

Finally, I thought. *The moment of truth is upon us.* There was a sense of finality, a feeling that the answers we sought were just beyond this threshold. As we prepared to enter, I steeled myself for whatever we might find. Luke Smith, whoever he was and whatever his role in this unfolding drama, would soon have nowhere left to hide.

❖

As we stood in the living room, the atmosphere was thick with tension and unspoken questions. Sarah, ever curious and impulsive, had already started to survey the surroundings, her hands itching to explore.

"Sarah!" I whispered sharply, catching her attention. She looked over her shoulder, her expression a mix of curiosity and mild defacement.

"Don't touch," I mouthed clearly, my frustration barely contained. *Why does she always have to fiddle with things?* I thought, a touch of exasperation colouring my thoughts. Gladys had asked us to wait while she supposedly went to fetch Jamie, and it hadn't taken Sarah more than a fleeting moment to succumb to her habitual nosiness.

"I don't see any dinner preparations," Sarah whispered back, her eyes scanning the room skeptically.

"No," I agreed, my gaze following hers. The lack of any culinary activity was just another red flag in a day full of them. "And I don't think that's the only thing Gladys is being untruthful about, either."

Sarah raised an eyebrow, intrigued.

Gladys returned then. "Jamie doesn't appear to be here," she announced. Her tone carried a hint of practiced shock, but I wasn't buying it. I had suspected there wouldn't be a Jamie waiting for us, but my suspicions about Luke's presence remained.

"Does Jamie live alone?" I asked, feigning ignorance. The question was strategic, designed to probe further into their living situation without revealing my hand.

"Um... no," Gladys replied, her voice tinged with uncertainty. "He has a partner."

"Oh," I responded, feigning surprise. "Is she about, then?" The deliberate misgendering was a ploy, an attempt to catch Gladys off guard and perhaps reveal more than she intended.

Gladys' face flushed a deep red, a clear indication that my question had hit a nerve.

"I'm sorry if I've embarrassed you," I said quickly, softening my approach. I needed Gladys cooperative, not defensive.

Gladys forced a smile. "His name is Luke," she corrected me. "But they have been having a few personal troubles lately, and Luke has gone to Melbourne for a few weeks to think things through."

"Oh, I see," I said calmly, although inside my mind was racing. This revelation added another layer of complexity to the case. *Who exactly is missing here? Jamie? Kain? Luke? Perhaps all of them, or maybe none.* The investigation was turning more convoluted by the minute. Each piece of information seemed to open up more avenues than it closed, and I couldn't shake the feeling that we were only scratching the surface of something much bigger.

"May I use the bathroom, please?" I asked politely.

"Sure," Gladys said. "It's just down the end of the hallway on the left."

I set off down the corridor, my footsteps muted against the carpet. The hallway felt narrow, almost claustrophobic, with walls adorned with an assortment of photographs that I noted for later perusal. As I walked, I overheard Sarah initiating her line of questioning. "So, what was it you said that Jamie was cooking again?" she asked Gladys. I couldn't help but shake my head slightly. Sarah's approach was often more direct than subtle, and I wondered if she realised how transparent her skepticism was.

Passing by the small toilet, I found myself drawn to the back corner bedroom. A hunch, fuelled by years of detective work, nudged me towards it. This room, I knew, contained black garbage bags piled inside. *Now, what are the chances of that?* I mused silently, a wry smile tugging at the corner of my mouth. *If I were to peek inside one of those bags, will I find something as sinister as a decomposing body, or is my imagination running wild?*

As I rounded the corner, just out of sight from the living room, I stole a quick glance back at Sarah and Gladys. Sarah might inadvertently push Gladys to the brink of hostility, but at least she would keep her occupied. This was my chance to investigate without interruption.

Leaning close to the bedroom door, I pressed my right ear against it, using my left index finger to block out the sounds of their conversation. All I could hear was silence, a deafening quiet that did nothing to ease the growing tension in my gut.

My palms, now slick with nervous perspiration, reached for the chrome door handle. I grasped it gently, careful not to make a sound. The metal felt cool and slightly damp against my skin, a stark contrast to the warmth radiating from my hand. I took a moment, steadying my breath, preparing myself for what I might find on the other side. Every sense was heightened, every nerve on edge.

Holding my breath, I gently nudged the door open, my movements cautious and deliberate. Every inch it opened felt like a mile, my heart pounding in sync with the slow reveal of the room's contents. The first black garbage bag came into view, and my mind raced with possibilities.

My curiosity overcame caution, and I pressed against the door with more force. It swung open wider, then suddenly bounced back towards me. The unexpected movement startled me, and in a moment of unguarded reaction, I pushed the door again. It halted abruptly, leaving a gap of about a foot and a half. "Fuck!" I muttered under my breath, my heart skipping a beat in frustration.

Gladys's voice, sharp and filled with anger, echoed down the hallway. "Hey! What the hell are you doing up there?" Her footsteps were quick and determined, approaching rapidly.

Startled, I felt a surge of adrenaline. There was an unsettling edge to this house, a tension that seemed to keep me constantly on edge. I couldn't put my finger on it, but something about this whole situation felt off.

As Gladys appeared, her face was a mix of fury and suspicion. "I think you'd better leave," she demanded, her tone brooking no argument.

Embarrassment mingled with my racing adrenaline. Part of me was desperate to know if Luke was hiding behind that door, yet I was also acutely aware of the delicate situation. We had pushed the boundaries of our welcome, and Gladys's demand to leave left little room for negotiation.

Reluctantly retreating from the bedroom, a whirlwind of thoughts and theories swirled in my head. *Was Luke concealed in that room, or was our pursuit leading us astray?* My determination, however, was unshaken. Every fibre of my being was committed to unraveling this enigma.

As I stepped back into the hallway, the atmosphere shifted abruptly. The lights flickered ominously, casting eerie shadows along the walls, and my radio crackled to life with static, breaking the tense silence. A chill ran down my spine, my senses on high alert.

Then, a whisper floated from the direction of the bedroom, barely audible yet chillingly clear. "Bye, Karl," it taunted, its tone dripping with smug triumph. Anger surged through me, hot and quick. That voice, that mocking farewell—it had to be Luke.

"You bastard!" I yelled and, driven by a mix of fury and adrenaline, I spun around and charged at the bedroom door with all my might. The door crashed open, slamming against the wall with force.

"Karl!" Sarah's voice was a mixture of shock and concern. "What the hell are you doing!?"

"He's here!" I shouted, my voice a cocktail of frustration and conviction. "Luke is here!"

Without hesitation, Sarah sprang into action. She drew her gun, her movements swift and decisive, as she barged past me into the room. Positioning herself strategically, she faced the doorway, her back to the large window, ready for any threat that might present itself. "Go! I've got you covered," she commanded, her tone laced with urgency.

I obeyed, stepping back and grabbing the door handle. In one swift motion, I slammed the door shut, narrowly missing Gladys's face as she appeared, a look of shock etched across her features.

"What the—" Sarah's voice trailed off in disbelief. We both stood there, our gazes locked on the unremarkable wall before us, its only notable feature now a sizeable dent from our forced entry.

I stood there, confused. I knew I had heard the voice. I just *knew* it. In a flurry of blurred emotions, I reached for the nearest garbage bag and ripped a great hole in its side. Rubbish spilled from its wound. Unsatisfied, I moved to the next bag and tore several large gashes through it as more rubbish began to spill out.

"Karl!" Sarah's voice cut through my frenzied actions, but it barely registered. My focus was singular – find Luke, prove he was here.

"I know he's here!" I bellowed, my hands tearing through another bag, rubbish spilling and spreading across the floor like the remnants of a defeated adversary.

"Karl!" Sarah yelled again, her voice sharper, more urgent this time. I felt her hand on my shoulder, trying to pull me back to reality, but I was too far gone. In a reflexive motion, I pushed her away, my arm striking her chest with more force than I had intended. She stumbled back, tripping over the rubbish-strewn floor. The sound of her head hitting the wall was horrific, a sickening crack that finally pierced my rage-induced fog.

I froze, staring in horror as Sarah slid down the wall. Her hand, cut by a shard of glass from the broken window, was bleeding profusely. Her firearm lay precariously on the floor, an ominous reminder of the danger I had put us both in.

"I'm sorry," I whispered, my voice barely audible. The gravity of my actions hit me like a physical blow, a wave of regret washing over me. The scene before me blurred with memories of a young Jamie struggling in a river, a haunting echo from my past.

In a daze of pain and regret, I left the house, my mind a chaotic blend of past and present. The questions, the doubts, the unresolved mysteries of both swirled together, clouding my judgment and overwhelming my usual composure.

I walked down the driveway, past our car, and continued aimlessly down the street. I was barely aware of Sarah driving past me later, her failure to stop a silent testament to the rift my actions had caused.

As I walked, the anger within me simmered and grew. The whisper, "Bye, Karl," replayed in my head, a mocking refrain that echoed my failure and fuelled my determination.

"I know I heard it," I said to myself, my voice a mix of anger and resolve. This wasn't the end. I couldn't let it be. The voice, the mystery, the unresolved threads of this case – I was determined to untangle them, no matter what it took.

❖

The walk back to my place felt endless, each step heavy with the weight of my actions and the unresolved mysteries swirling in my head. The city was shrouded in darkness by the time I arrived home, the night sky a blanket of inky blackness, mirroring my tumultuous thoughts.

My phone buzzed repeatedly with calls from Sarah and Sergeant Claiborne, but I couldn't face them, not yet. The guilt over Sarah's injury and the frustration from the case were too raw, too fresh. I needed time to process, to think.

First, I tended to Jargus, my steadfast companion. His presence was a small comfort in the storm of my emotions. Ensuring his bowl was filled with food, I then mechanically changed into my black sweatpants and a sleeveless muscle tee, my movements automatic, devoid of the usual purpose.

I found myself drawn back to my car, almost subconsciously. Parking under the familiar gum trees, their leaves rustling harshly in the strengthening wind, I settled in. The wind's howl seemed to echo the turmoil inside me, a fitting soundtrack to my restless vigil.

I sat there, watching, waiting. My eyes were fixed on the dark, silent house that held so many answers I sought. The quiet was oppressive, the darkness impenetrable. But I remained, a sentinel in the night, driven by a mixture of duty and an unyielding need for closure.

The hours passed, marked only by the occasional flicker of streetlights or the distant bark of a dog. My patience yielded nothing but the stillness of the night and the unanswered questions that hung in the air like a thick fog.

As the night wore on, my mind replayed the day's events, each memory a piece of the puzzle I was desperate to solve. The whispered "Bye, Karl," the torn garbage bags, Sarah's injury – they all swirled in my head, refusing to coalesce into a coherent picture. I knew I couldn't give up, not when the answers were still out there, lurking in the shadows of this dark, silent house.

4338.211

(30 July 2018)

THE OWENS

4338.211.1

A few hours earlier, the call had disrupted the monotony of my restless thoughts. A distressed neighbour had reported not seeing Karen or Chris Owen for several days. Initially, the call didn't strike me as particularly unusual. Cases like these weren't typically in my wheelhouse.

The Owens were well-known figures in Tasmania, their commitment to environmental conservation and the preservation of our state's natural beauty earning them widespread respect. Their frequent travels across Tasmania for various environmental projects meant their absence from home wasn't necessarily alarming. I had considered delegating the initial check to a standard patrol unit, but then a crucial detail caught my attention.

The neighbour had reported "disturbing activity" at the Owens' residence, including multiple deliveries by a small truck. The mention of a small truck piqued my interest, especially since it wasn't the first time such a detail had surfaced in recent missing persons reports. This coincidence couldn't be ignored, so I decided that Sarah and I should take a closer look.

Now, as I sat in my car, gripping the steering wheel, my gaze drifted to the sky. Fluffy white clouds lazily drifted across the sun, their passing casting transient shadows over the landscape. It was a serene, almost idyllic sight, but to my left, the tranquility was being overshadowed by the approach of darker, more menacing clouds. They moved quickly, foreboding in their intensity, heralding the imminent arrival of a storm.

Turning to Sarah, I spoke with a sense of urgency. "We'd better make quick work of this investigation," I said. "I don't think we have much time before it hits." My words were not just about the approaching storm but also about the sense of impending urgency in the case. The Owens' disappearance, the small truck, the storm rolling in – it all felt interconnected, pieces of a larger puzzle that we needed to solve swiftly. The atmosphere was charged, not just with the impending storm, but with the anticipation of uncovering something significant in our investigation.

Sarah's silent nod was a stark reminder of the tension lingering between us since my uncharacteristic outburst at the Smith house. The regret over my actions weighed heavily on me, but the complexities of this case, with its echoes of past experiences and unresolved threads, seemed to cloud my judgment. *Was it the presence of Luke that unsettled me, or the resurgence of memories related to my days with Jamie?* I hadn't quite figured it out.

Our drive was abruptly interrupted as Sarah suddenly cried out, "Watch out!" Her hand instinctively reached towards the wheel. Reacting swiftly, I slammed on the brakes, narrowly avoiding several brown chickens that had scurried onto the road.

Looking at Sarah, I noticed her struggle to suppress a smile at the absurdity of the situation. "We must be getting close," I remarked, trying to lighten the mood.

"We are," she confirmed, pointing to a nearby street sign. "That's the road to the Owens' property."

I beeped the horn, hoping to hasten the hens across the road. Yet, the last hen, trailing behind her companions, seemed in no hurry. She gazed up at me with beady, defiant eyes, unaffected by the horn's blare. It was as if she was reproaching me for the disturbance. Unhurriedly, she continued her way, pecking at the ground after every few steps.

"This is ridiculous," Sarah exclaimed, her frustration evident as she opened her car door to intervene.

I couldn't help but chuckle as I watched Sarah attempt to shoo the chickens off the road. They had obviously strayed from a nearby yard and now, amusingly, several seemed inclined to follow her back to the car.

I rolled down the window. "You shoo, I'll drive," I called out, laughter in my voice.

"Fine," she responded, slightly exasperated.

Driving cautiously, I navigated past the hens and pulled up a few car lengths ahead. As Sarah walked back towards the car, the scene became almost comical. The determined hens seemed hell-bent on giving us a hard time.

"Karl! Wait!" Sarah's voice rang out, her tone a mix of amusement and frustration. I was driving slowly up the road, trying to avoid any more chicken-related delays. But as Sarah picked up her pace, the hens seemed equally determined to keep up with her. The sight was almost surreal – Sarah running, the chickens in pursuit, and me at the wheel, laughter bubbling up uncontrollably. This absurd chicken chase provided a brief, much-needed respite from the gravity of our investigation.

As I steered the car onto the laneway leading to the Owens' property, I slowed down to let Sarah catch up. The hens, thankfully, had lost interest in their chase once she left the main road.

"I think the girls like you," I teased Sarah as she climbed back into the car, trying to maintain the lighter mood for just a bit longer.

"Not funny, Karl! There's a reason I don't do country," she retorted, shooting me a glare that seemed to expect my understanding of her aversion.

"Sarah, you were born in the outback," I reminded her playfully. "That's more country than country."

"That doesn't mean I liked it," she huffed back, her demeanour a mixture of irritation and amusement.

I couldn't help but chuckle at her reaction. "That's not what your brother says," I added, nudging her playfully with the memory of her past.

Her response was immediate – a swift punch to my shoulder. "Just drive," she commanded, though the corner of her mouth twitched, betraying her amusement.

We continued along the laneway, which soon gave way to a narrow dirt road. The car jostled uncomfortably, bouncing over an uneven mix of pebbles, rocks, and potholes. Dense native forest flanked the road, its thick foliage obscuring any view beyond the immediate path ahead and the road we had left behind.

Sarah's exclamation broke the silence as we emerged onto a spacious clearing. "Oh my God!" she gasped, taking in the sight before us.

The Owens' cottage was a picture of rural charm. Small and simple, the stone-and-cedar structure exuded a quaint beauty. It was modest in size, likely no more than three bedrooms, but it stood proudly against its backdrop. The varying shades of green from the surrounding forest enhanced its appeal, lending it an almost storybook quality.

Sarah's reaction to the cottage was a mixture of awe and nostalgia. As she stepped out of the car, she stood for a moment, just taking in the sight of the humble yet captivating structure. Its rustic charm seemed to transport her to another place.

"Bringing back memories?" I teased, unable to resist the opportunity for a lighthearted jab, my grin widening as I observed her reaction.

Her response was a beautiful, radiant smile that seemed to light up her entire face. Sarah's eyes, a striking shade of green, sparkled with a joy and warmth that was infectious. It was moments like these, amidst the seriousness of our work, that reminded me of the lighter, more human side of my partner.

Suddenly, Sarah's attention shifted. "Look!" she exclaimed, pointing towards a group of small potoroos nibbling on the long grass by a large barn off to the left of the cottage. Her fascination was evident as she began to move towards them, her approach gentle and unthreatening. Her fingers clicked softly, and her voice, carried by the wind, was soothing and inviting, coaxing the shy creatures to trust her.

I watched, momentarily captivated by the scene, a brief respite from the intensity of our investigation. However, the reality of our situation quickly pulled me back. We had a job to do, and as much as I wanted to indulge in the peacefulness of the moment, duty called.

The radio crackled to life, breaking the tranquility. "CITY632. Are you there? Over," the voice from dispatch cut through the quiet.

I reached back into the car, grabbing the radio. "CITY632. We're at the Owens' property now. Over," I responded, shifting back into professional mode.

The dispatcher's next words heightened the sense of urgency. "CITY632. The neighbour who called this morning has just called back. She is pretty shaken. Said there was a lot of activity at the property. Went quiet about thirty minutes ago."

"Copy that, dispatch," I confirmed into the radio, my voice embodying the resolve and concentration that the situation demanded. "We'll proceed with caution." I clipped the radio back into place, my mind already racing through various scenarios we might encounter.

Surveying the Owens' property, I noted how it was enveloped by dense forest. The isolation was striking, the nearest neighbour residing hundreds of meters away. This only deepened the mystery of the neighbour's call – *how could they have observed so much from such a distance?*

Lost in thought, I was startled when I noticed Sarah already prepared for whatever might lie ahead, her firearm at the ready. "For once, you're actually right about the gun," I muttered, almost to myself. I unholstered my own weapon, feeling its familiar weight in my hand. "Follow my lead," I instructed, trying to mask the unease that the situation evoked.

Together, we moved stealthily towards the cottage's front veranda. I took the direct approach, heading for the steps, while Sarah veered left. My heart raced as the first step creaked loudly under my weight, a stark reminder of the need for silence and stealth.

Suddenly, Sarah's whisper broke my concentration, causing my next step to land with an even louder thud. I turned to see her crouched in the flowerbed, an action that initially baffled me. *What is she doing?*

Sarah held up a small bunch of white daisies. "These look like they've been freshly picked," she said. "They were lying on the edge of the decking here." She pointed toward where she had found the bunch.

"Daisies?" I asked, my mind trying to piece together their significance.

"Yeah," Sarah replied. "It's a bit odd. Maybe the neighbour was right. There were people here earlier. Do you think they're still around?"

I paused, considering her words. "Not sure," I admitted. The silence that enveloped the property suggested abandonment, yet the daisies indicated recent human activity. "Why don't you go check out the barn?"

"Yeah, alright," she agreed, her tone business-like as she prepared to investigate further.

As she walked away, I felt a surge of protective instinct. "Sarah," I called out in a hushed yet urgent whisper. A myriad of sarcastic remarks flitted through my mind, but I settled on a sincere caution instead. "Be careful," I said.

She nodded, acknowledging my concern. As Sarah disappeared into the distance, her figure blending with the shadows as she approached the barn, I turned back to the cottage, steeling myself for what lay ahead. My trust in Sarah's abilities was absolute, but the unpredictable nature of our current case left a knot of anxiety in my stomach.

I gazed up at the steps leading to the front door, trying to steady my nerves. "Only three more to go," I murmured under my breath, psyching myself up for what could be on the other side.

Reaching the final step, I noticed the front door was slightly ajar. My pulse quickened. *Is someone still inside, or had they fled in haste?* The possibilities raced through my mind, each scenario more unsettling than the last.

"Hello? Police!" I called out, nudging the door further open with a gentle tap of my foot. The silence that greeted me was almost as disconcerting as a response would have been.

"Hello? Police!" I called out again, louder this time, announcing my intention to enter. "I'm coming in." With caution, I pushed the door wide open and stepped inside, my gun leading the way.

The narrow hallway was shrouded in a quiet that felt almost oppressive. Every step I took was deliberate, my ears straining for any sound of movement. But the silence remained unbroken.

Entering the master bedroom, I was greeted by an empty, almost barren room. The bed was stripped of sheets and blankets, giving the space a desolate feel. The open mahogany wardrobe stood as a silent testament to a hurried departure, its contents sparse. I lowered my gun slightly, the immediate sense of threat ebbing away. It seemed evident that the Owens were away, perhaps on one of their environmental excursions.

Moving on, I entered the kitchen, which was small but tidy. A peek inside the fridge confirmed my suspicions - it was nearly as empty as the wardrobe. They weren't here. The mystery of the slightly open door lingered in my mind, but it didn't seem to be connected to our current investigation. Perhaps it was indeed a case for local police or a curious neighbour to ponder over.

The urgency to refocus on finding Jamie gnawed at me as I moved through the Owens' cottage. This side investigation, though necessary, felt like a detour from our main objective. The distant rumble of thunder echoed my growing restlessness, a reminder of the brewing storm outside and the tumultuous nature of our case.

As I stood in the kitchen, a loud thunderclap shattered the silence, jolting me into high alert. Instinctively, my gun came up, ready for any threat. "Is anyone there?" I called out, my voice steady but loud enough to carry through the cottage. Moving cautiously from the kitchen to the dining room, I kept my focus sharp, my eyes scanning every inch of the space ahead.

Navigating through the cramped dining area, I noted the odd placement of a large, overflowing bookcase filled with various science books. It struck me as peculiar, yet fitting for the Owens, who were known for their unconventional ways.

My concentration broke for a split second as my elbow inadvertently brushed against a slim scientific journal on the dining table, sending it tumbling to the floor. Papers flew out, creating a whispering swish as they floated to the ground.

Crouching down carefully, still mindful of my surroundings, I reached for the journal and the papers. As I did so, my finger brushed against something wet on the floor. Straightening up, I examined my fingertip, now smeared with a reddish fluid. "Blood!" I gasped, a surge of adrenaline shooting through me as I realised the potential danger I was in.

My eyes quickly traced the small drops of blood that started near the dining table, following a trail that snaked through the lounge and ended near the coffee table. The droplets appeared dry, indicating they had been there for some time, possibly around forty-eight hours. *But why was the first drop still wet?*

As I followed the blood trail to the coffee table, my heart pounded in my chest. The fear of finding a body, the first casualty in our investigation, loomed over me. I reached the end of the trail, my eyes searching desperately for any sign of a struggle or further clues. But there was nothing – no signs of violence, no more blood, just an ominous silence that hung heavily in the air.

The mystery deepened. The dried blood suggested an incident had occurred days ago, yet the fresh drop hinted at something more recent. The puzzle was complex, the pieces not quite fitting together. I stood there, my mind racing, trying to piece together the clues in front of me. *What had happened here? And did it connect to our search for Jamie?* The answers felt just out of reach, hidden within the walls of this seemingly tranquil cottage.

The next thunderclap, much closer and more menacing than before, yanked my attention away from the mysterious blood trail. Peering out the window, I saw how the sky had transformed into an ominous canvas of dark, roiling clouds. It seemed to mirror the growing unease I felt inside.

Then, cutting through the growing storm, a scream pierced the air, chilling and desperate. It was followed almost instantly by the sharp, unmistakable sound of a gunshot. My heart leapt into my throat.

"Sarah!" The name tore from my lips as I raced toward the front door, all thoughts of caution abandoned. Adrenaline surged through me, propelling me forward with singular focus.

I burst out of the cottage, leaping off the veranda and hitting the ground running. I skipped the steps entirely, my mind only on Sarah. The fear that something might have happened to her was overwhelming.

I sprinted toward the barn, desperate to find her. But my heart sank when I saw the padlocked door. "Shit!" I cursed aloud, frantically searching for another entry point. The thought of Sarah in danger was unbearable. I couldn't let anything happen to her; the guilt would be insurmountable.

Rounding the final corner of the barn, I spotted her. She was sitting among the tall reeds by a small, spring-fed dam. "Sarah!" I called out again, dread and fear mixing with relief as I ran toward her. My mind was racing with horrific scenarios, each one more terrifying than the last.

As I neared her, Sarah turned her head, her face streaked with tears, her expression one of shock and despair.

I skidded to a halt, my heart dropping at the sight before me. Beside her lay a small, motionless body in the reeds, a pool of blood slowly expanding from a single bullet wound in the chest. "Ahh. Shit, Sarah," I whispered, my voice barely audible over the pounding of my heart.

The scene was a nightmare come to life. The realisation of what had happened, the gravity of the situation, hit me like a physical blow. This investigation had taken a tragic and unforeseen turn, one that would undoubtedly leave an indelible mark on both of us. I stood there, rooted to the spot, struggling to process the scene before me, the weight of the tragedy settling heavily upon my shoulders.

"I didn't mean to," Sarah murmured, her voice breaking as she wiped another tear from her eyes. The remorse in her tone was palpable, and despite my frustration, I couldn't help but feel a pang of sympathy for her.

I reached out and grabbed Sarah by the arm, helping her to her feet. The situation was absurd, almost surreal. "You just shot their goose!" I exclaimed, my voice a mix of disbelief and irritation.

"It was an accident! She flew at me. I swear she was coming for my face," Sarah defended herself, her voice tinged with a mix of distress and defensiveness. The oddity of the situation did little to alleviate the tension.

I looked at her, my frustration clearly written on my face. "Do you have any idea how much paperwork this is going to be?" I asked, though it was more of a rhetorical question, a venting of my exasperation at the situation.

Sarah's expression soured even more. "I could have been seriously injured," she retorted, her tone sharp.

"Well, at least you wouldn't be dead," I responded, gesturing towards the lifeless goose at our feet, my comment a mix of dry humour and pointed reality.

"You can be a real insensitive bastard sometimes, Karl!" Sarah snapped, her patience clearly worn thin by the events. With that, she turned and stormed off towards the car.

I stood there, watching her go, and took a deep, slow breath, trying to calm the whirlwind of emotions swirling inside me. Another breath followed, a bit steadier this time.

"Sarah, wait!" I called out after her, but she didn't stop, her stride purposeful and angry.

"There's blood in the house," I yelled, hoping this piece of information would get her attention.

Sarah paused and turned slightly. "And a body?" she asked, her voice carrying a mix of hope and dread.

I shook my head in response. "No. Just this goose," I replied, giving the unfortunate bird a slight nudge with my foot.

"I'll go call for forensics," Sarah declared, her voice still laced with frustration as she resumed her walk to the car.

Watching her leave, I couldn't help but feel a mix of regret and concern. The tension between us had escalated, and the situation with the goose, bizarre as it was, had only added to the strain. I hoped that, in time, we could move past this and refocus on the search for Jamie and Luke. But for now, I was left standing by the lifeless goose, pondering the absurd twists and turns our investigation had taken.

THE CHASE

4338.211.2

As I trudged toward the patrol car, large drops of rain splattered against the ground, seemingly in sync with my mood. The sky, once a mottled canvas of darkening clouds, now seemed to openly express its displeasure. *Great. Now even the sky's mad at me,* I mused ruefully.

"Karl, we have to go!" Sarah's voice, full of urgency, broke through my thoughts.

"What is it?" I called back, slowing my pace slightly. Sarah's energy was almost infectious, but her anger could be equally compelling. I always marvelled at how she managed to maintain such vigour, especially when she was upset.

"A priority call has just come over the radio, two cars are driving at high speed just off the highway near Collinsvale. We're the closest unit. Quick, let's go!" she explained, her arms waving frantically, urging me to hurry.

"We can't just leave the scene here," I began, feeling a responsibility to maintain our current investigation. But Sarah was already several steps ahead.

"It'll be fine. I've already notified dispatch and forensics are on their way. We can swing by afterwards to check up on things. This call is urgent," she interrupted, her tone leaving no room for debate.

"Fine," I acquiesced with a grimace, quickening my pace to the driver's side. Sarah had already started the ignition by the time I reached the car. "Shift over, I'll drive," I instructed firmly, motioning for her to move to the passenger seat.

I watched as Sarah clambered over the centre console, settling into the passenger seat with a huff. Her sense of urgency was palpable, a clear indication of the seriousness of the call.

"Come on then!" she urged, her impatience evident.

Sliding into the driver's seat, I didn't hesitate. I slammed my foot down on the accelerator, feeling the immediate response of the patrol car's powerful V8 engine. The vehicle roared to life, a beast unleashed, as we sped down the long dirt driveway. The car fishtailed slightly, struggling for traction on the rain-slicked earth, but I held firm, controlling the vehicle with practiced ease.

The adrenaline of the chase began to replace the frustration and tension of the previous events. As the car surged forward, cutting through the rain, I felt a renewed focus. The urgency of the new call demanded all my attention, and I was ready to rise to the challenge, leaving the bizarre events at the Owens' cottage behind, if only for a moment.

Sarah's smile, a rare sight since the goose incident, reflected the excitement of the chase. She swiftly picked up the radio, her voice steady and clear. "CITY632 requesting an update on the two speeding cars sighted near Collinsvale."

The dispatcher's response came promptly. "Copy that CITY632. We already had a Polair chopper in the air. They're looking for the vehicles now. What is your location?"

I brought the patrol car to a halt at the end of the Owens' driveway, where it intersected with the main road. The choice was stark: head back towards Glenorchy or delve deeper into Collinsvale. The decision hinged on the exact location of the speeding cars.

"CITY632. We're at the edge of the Owens' property in Collinsvale," Sarah reported back to dispatch, her eyes scanning the road ahead. The rain was intensifying, reducing visibility, blurring the world outside into a watery haze.

"Copy that, CITY632. The chopper has sight of the vehicles. They should be coming—" The dispatcher's voice was drowned out as two vehicles suddenly zoomed past us, heading in the direction of Collinsvale. They flew by so fast, a spray of water fanned out behind them, momentarily obscuring our view.

My pulse quickened as I gripped the steering wheel tighter. Without hesitation, I stepped hard on the accelerator and swung the car onto the main road. The patrol car's rear wheels lost traction for a brief moment, sending us into a controlled power slide. The thrill of the pursuit ignited within me, a small grin creeping onto my face as we joined the chase. Sarah, ever the professional, activated the flashing lights and siren, the familiar sounds adding to the intensity of the moment.

"We have a visual. In pursuit now," Sarah reported into the radio. The wipers worked furiously, struggling against the relentless downpour.

"Copy that, CITY632," the dispatcher replied, their voice a calm constant amid the storm and adrenaline.

The patrol car's tires screeched in protest as I navigated the sharp corner at breakneck speed, the rain-soaked road adding an extra layer of danger to our pursuit. "Do we know who the drivers are?" I asked Sarah, keeping my eyes fixed on the road ahead, trying to close the gap between us and the speeding cars.

"Let's find out," Sarah responded, her voice steady as she relayed the question into the radio.

"Negative, CITY632. Are you able to get a visual on a number plate?" the dispatcher asked.

I leaned forward in my seat, squinting through the windshield. The relentless downpour made it nearly impossible to see anything clearly. "I can't make it out. Can you?" I asked Sarah, hoping her angle might offer a better view.

"Me neither," she replied, her voice tinged with frustration. "You'll have to get us a little closer. Watch out for the spray from the cars." Her earlier excitement had shifted to a palpable sense of seriousness as the dangerous reality of our high-speed chase became more apparent.

Pushing the accelerator further, I felt the car surge forward. My head nearly grazed the roof as we flew over a slight rise in the road, the patrol car's rear wheels briefly losing traction. I managed to maintain control, silently thanking the countless hours spent in advanced driver training courses.

"Shit, Karl," Sarah exclaimed as she braced herself against the car's interior, preventing a collision with the side window.

"Well, did you get it?" I asked, my voice filled with a mix of anxiety and determination. Despite the thrill of the chase, the worsening weather conditions were a growing concern. The rain made every manoeuvre more perilous, and I was acutely aware of the police policy to terminate pursuits if they became too risky. *Just another minute or two*, I thought. *We can at least give it that.*

"Yeah," Sarah answered, her fingers working quickly. "I'm running it through the system now."

I glanced at the screen beside me, hoping for a quick result. But each time my eyes darted to it, all I saw was the word 'processing', a blinking reminder of the wait. My grip on the wheel tightened as we continued the pursuit, the chase becoming more treacherous with every passing second. The sense of urgency was palpable, a silent but constant pressure as we raced against time and the elements, hoping for a breakthrough before we were forced to back off.

As the pursuit continued, the two vehicles we were chasing skilfully manoeuvred along the winding hillside of Collinsvale Road, eventually turning onto Collins Cap Road. The chase was intense, every turn a high-speed ballet of danger and precision. Then, unexpectedly, the cars made a sharp turn onto Springdale Road.

"Looks like they're looping back," I noted, a hint of surprise in my voice. I slammed on the brakes, the patrol car's tires protesting against the sudden deceleration.

"What are you doing?" Sarah's voice was tinged with desperation, her eagerness to continue the pursuit palpable.

"We're going back. The distance is shorter and we can cut them off when they arrive at the intersection," I explained quickly. I shifted the car into reverse, my mind calculating the best route to intercept the suspects. With a swift motion, I yanked the handbrake, sending the car into a controlled spin before shifting back into drive and accelerating forward.

"Jeez, Karl!" Sarah exclaimed, gripping the dashboard and door handle for stability as the car spun and regained its direction.

The radio crackled to life again. "CITY632," the dispatcher said. "The chopper has you in sight. You are still in front of them. If you're quick, you'll cut them off. Other units are preparing a spike strip at the end of Glenlusk Road as a precaution."

"Copy that," Sarah responded, her voice steady as she relayed our position and intentions back to dispatch.

As we neared the intersection with Springdale Road, Sarah suddenly cried out, "Shit!"

"What is it?" I asked, my foot easing off the accelerator, bringing the vehicle to a stop in the middle of the intersection.

Sarah's next words hit me like a bolt of lightning. "The rego check found a match. It's Gladys Cramer!"

"Gladys!" I echoed, my mind racing. "Are you sure?"

"Positive," she confirmed, her voice filled with conviction. "I mean, I could have misread the plate, but seriously, the odds of a misread returning a person of interest like this would be insane!"

The revelation sent a shockwave through me. Gladys Cramer, a key figure in our ongoing investigation, was now the prime suspect in a high-speed chase. The coincidence was too significant to ignore. My hands tightened on the steering wheel, a mixture of anticipation and disbelief coursing through me. This case had taken another unexpected turn, and we were right in the thick of it. With renewed focus, I prepared to reengage in the pursuit, the stakes now higher than ever.

The minutes ticked by agonisingly slow, the constant drumming of the rain on the car roof adding to the tense atmosphere. My concern escalated with each passing moment. *The cars should have reached us by now*. The thought of a potential crash, compounded by the treacherous weather, sent a shiver down my spine. Yet, I clung to the hope that if such a tragedy had occurred, the chopper would have informed us.

Suddenly, a sharp, high-pitched sound erupted from the car radio, startling both of us. "Aargh!" we shouted in unison, instinctively covering our ears.

"What the fuck was that!?" Sarah exclaimed, her voice echoing my own shock and confusion.

"CITY632," Dispatch's voice came through, breaking the momentary chaos, "the vehicles have turned down Myrtle Forest Road. The chopper has lost a visual on them."

"Shit!" I yelled, frustration boiling over. I slammed my foot down on the accelerator, the patrol car lurching forward as we raced down Springdale Road towards Myrtle Forest.

"I don't understand," Sarah said, her voice tinged with confusion. "Where are they? How could the chopper have lost them?"

"I don't know," I responded, equally perplexed. The area was remote, with limited road options, most of which ended in dead-ends. The thought that the drivers might have intentionally turned down one of these roads seemed reckless, even desperate.

As we reached the end of the bitumen road, I braked hard, the car skidding slightly on the wet surface. Our only option now was to continue on foot through the dense forest.

I grabbed the radio from Sarah. "This is CITY632. Do you have a visual on the vehicles again?" I asked, a sense of urgency evident in my voice.

"CITY632. No. There is no visual on either car," the dispatcher responded, their words confirming our worst fears.

"Fuck," I yelled, a mix of anger and helplessness overwhelming me. I pounded my fists against the steering wheel in frustration. We were so close, yet now, it felt like we were back to square one. The suspects had vanished, and with them, our lead on Gladys Cramer. The weight of the situation, the missed opportunities, and the relentless rain all seemed to converge, creating a storm of emotions within me. I knew we had to regroup and figure out our next move, but in that moment, all I could feel was the bitter sting of frustration.

Stepping out of the patrol car into the relentless downpour, I was immediately soaked to the bone. The rain was unyielding, a physical manifestation of the frustrations and challenges we were facing. Sarah, undeterred by the weather, followed me out. I stood there for a moment, hands clasped behind my head, feeling the rain cascade down my face, drenching my clothes, mirroring the turmoil inside me.

"Karl, check this out," Sarah's voice cut through the sound of the rain.

I trudged across the muddy, wet gravel towards her, slipping slightly with each step. There was no need to ask what she had found; it was blatantly obvious. Two fresh sets of tyre treads were imprinted deeply in the mud, a clear sign of recent activity. My eyes traced the path of the tracks, my body instinctively following.

"Well, this doesn't make sense," I muttered, examining the first set of treads. I glanced over at Sarah, noting how the rain had plastered her hair to her face, adding a visible element of misery to our already bleak situation.

"These tyre tracks look like the vehicle didn't even stop. How can they just end here? It's as though the car just disappeared," Sarah questioned, her voice filled with confusion and disbelief.

My gaze shifted to the large, wooden toilet block standing ominously in front of us. "I don't know," I replied softly, my voice barely above a murmur. I scrutinised the structure. "There wouldn't be much left of that wall if they'd driven into it."

The situation was puzzling. The tracks led directly to the toilet block, yet there was no sign of impact, no debris, nothing to indicate that the vehicles had collided with the structure. It was as if they had simply vanished into thin air. My mind raced through possibilities, but none seemed to fit.

"There's still this second set of tracks," Sarah yelled out, pointing at them. We both instinctively ducked as a loud clap of thunder rolled through the sky, sending the rain falling even heavier. "Where do you reckon they lead to?" Sarah yelled over the din of the storm as I drew closer to inspect the tracks.

"Well, they can't go too far out here," I observed, my voice raised to be heard over the thunder. I examined the path of the tracks. "They break away from the first set down here and then veer to the right. It looks like they head to the back of the toilet block."

I didn't need to signal Sarah; her instinct had already kicked in. She was swiftly following the trail, waving at me to catch up. "It's here!" she called out, her voice tinged with a mix of excitement and urgency.

"Shit!" I muttered under my breath, quickening my pace to join her. As I approached, I saw what had caught her attention: a car with its passenger side door left wide open. Cautiously, I moved towards the car, my senses on high alert, as Sarah followed, her gun drawn and ready.

"They must have taken off on foot," I shouted through the rain, scanning the area for any sign of the drivers. "There's nobody here."

Another thunderclap echoed, merging with the sound of the storm. As it faded into the distance, a sharp clang rang out, startlingly close, from the direction of the toilet block.

Sarah instantly pointed her gun towards the small building, her posture tense and alert. The toilet block, nestled in a small clearing, was about ten meters from the forest's edge. Two large myrtle trees flanked its sides, their branches scraping against the tin roof in the growing wind.

With my gun drawn and at the ready, I signalled for Sarah to cover me as we approached the toilet block. The tension was palpable, each step deliberate and cautious. "Police!" I called out authoritatively. "Come out slowly with your hands up." My voice echoed against the concrete walls, swallowed by the storm's cacophony.

Another thunderclap boomed directly overhead, almost in response to my command. It was quickly followed by another metallic clang from within the toilet block, heightening our alertness.

I indicated to Sarah that I was going in first. Glancing up, I noted the unisex sign on the entrance – a small detail, but it meant there would only be one room to clear. Simplicity was a small blessing in situations like this.

Gun leading the way, I rounded the corner into the interior of the block. The dim lighting cast eerie shadows across the walls. Water dripped steadily from a small hole in the ceiling, the sound unnervingly loud in the otherwise silent space. The interior was surprisingly spacious for just two cubicles, the farthest one ominously closed. I gestured towards it, silently communicating its presence to Sarah as she stepped in behind me.

I slid along the wall, my movements slow and calculated. Peering into the first cubicle, I found it empty. I signalled to Sarah, who nodded in understanding. The tension was like a physical force pressing in on us.

Just then, the wind howled through a gap in the roof, and another peal of thunder resounded above. The dim light flickered ominously several times before plunging us into complete darkness. Reacting quickly, I pulled out my flashlight and held it under my gun, casting a narrow beam of light ahead.

A spectrum of colours danced under the door of the closed cubicle. My skin prickled with a mix of anticipation and dread. Outside, the car radio crackled loudly, a dissonant accompaniment to the storm and our tense situation.

The adrenaline-fuelled moment I kicked in the door of the corner cubicle was a blur. The door snapped open with a violent swing, revealing a glimpse of a crouched woman with long, silver hair before it shut again, plunging the room into darkness. In that fleeting glimpse, a spark of recognition flickered across my mind, but I couldn't immediately place it.

Frozen by the brief encounter, I stood motionless, unable to process what I had just seen. Sarah, ever decisive, stepped in front of me and pushed the door open with her foot, her gun at the ready.

"It's empty," Sarah announced, her voice tinged with surprise. She turned to look at me, her expression puzzled by my lack of response.

"What the fuck's up with you?" Sarah asked as we stepped back into the rain. "You look like you've seen a ghost."

I remained silent, my mind racing, trying to make sense of the fleeting image I had seen.

The radio's crackle broke through my reverie. "CITY632. Are you there?" the voice called.

I hurried back to the patrol car, slipping in the muddy terrain. "CITY632 here. Go ahead," I said, almost growling into the radio as I threw open the door and grabbed the handset.

"CITY632. Still no sightings of either car. Patrols will remain on alert for the next few hours. Over."

"Copy that. We have located one of the vehicles. We are here with it at the start of Myrtle Creek Forest. Looks like it has been abandoned," I reported back, still trying to shake off the unsettling feeling from the toilet block encounter.

"Copy that, CITY632, patrols are on their way."

"Understood. CITY632 out."

I sat in the driver's seat, my gaze fixed on the toilet block, lost in thought. The decision to wait for the additional patrols and leave the scene to forensics felt like the only logical move. My mind was still reeling from the mysterious figure in the toilet block and the unreal sense of recognition.

"Come on then," I called to Sarah, urging her to join me in the car, away from the relentless rain.

As Sarah paused at the passenger side of the car, her attention caught by something in the distance, I tried to discern what had captivated her. She was staring intently towards the trees where the walking trail began, but from my vantage point, I couldn't make out anything unusual.

Sarah tapped on the side of the car and waved for me to get out.

Her tap on the car and gesture to join her piqued my curiosity. "What is it?" I asked, stepping out into the relentless rain again. "Let's just wait in the car, this rain doesn't look like it's letting up any time soon."

"I think I've found something," Sarah replied, a hint of excitement in her voice. She moved towards the entrance sign of Myrtle Forest Walk, deftly avoiding the growing puddles.

"What am I supposed to be looking at?" I asked, following her with a mix of curiosity and skepticism.

"This!" Sarah exclaimed triumphantly, holding up a small bracelet she had picked up from the ground. "And these footprints in the mud are fresh," she added, her voice tinged with the thrill of discovery.

"Those footprints could belong to anyone," I countered, trying to remain pragmatic despite the mounting evidence.

"But I don't think this does," she retorted, thrusting the bracelet in front of my face. The initials "G.C." were engraved inside it.

My skepticism faltered as I looked at the bracelet. *Perhaps Sarah is right*, I considered, the possibility dawning on me.

"I'll go call it in," she announced, turning to head back to the car.

"No," I responded instinctively, grabbing her arm to stop her. She looked at me, surprised by my abruptness. "Not yet," I said, releasing my grip.

Sarah shook her arm, readjusting her jacket sleeve with a flick of her wrist. Then, without a word, she headed down the walking trail.

"Sarah!" I called after her, my voice laced with frustration. "Let's wait for the other patrols to arrive." But she didn't stop, determined to follow the new lead.

I let out a sigh, torn between protocol and the urge to follow the trail of clues Sarah had discovered. After a moment's hesitation, I decided to chase after her. The rain, the mud, the unanswered questions – none of it mattered now. We were on the cusp of a breakthrough, and I couldn't let Sarah go it alone.

❖

As we trudged along the forest trail, the minutes stretched out endlessly. With each step, I scanned the dense woods to either side, looking for any sign of Gladys. Despite our efforts, the feeling of futility began to set in. Finally, I had to call a halt.

"Sarah!" I called out, but she continued forward, undeterred. Frustrated, I chased after her. "Sarah, stop it! This is madness!" I shouted, my voice tinged with desperation. "If Gladys is out here, we're never going to find her," I reasoned, hoping to bring some sense to our seemingly fruitless endeavour.

"Why won't we find her?" Sarah shot back, her voice sharp with emotion.

"There's too much forest. It's raining, cold and muddy. We're just two people out here," I explained, reaching out to turn her towards me. It was then I noticed her distress.

My concern deepened as I saw tears rolling down her face. "What's wrong?" I asked, my voice softening.

"Nothing," she replied hastily, her hands wiping at her wet face.

Her response didn't match her expression, but I knew pressing her for answers wasn't the right approach at the moment. Gently, I cupped my hands around her face, looking into her eyes. In a moment of shared vulnerability, I pulled her close, wrapping my arms around her. It was a gesture of comfort, a reassurance that we were in this together.

"Thank you, Karl," Sarah murmured softly, her head resting against my chest. We stood there, enveloped in the steady rhythm of the rain, lost in a moment of quiet solidarity.

UNSATISFIED

4338.211.3

"Well, don't you two look like shit," Sergeant Claiborne announced as I walked in, Sarah falling through the doorway behind me.

Ignoring his comment, I got straight to the point. "Sergeant," I began, "I'd like to request an unmarked car to stakeout Gladys Cramer's house. Just in case she goes home tonight."

His immediate "No," without even glancing up from his papers, caught me off guard. My frustration, simmering just below the surface from the day's events, began to boil over.

"No?" I echoed, my voice betraying my irritation.

"That's right. No," he repeated, still engrossed in his paperwork.

"But why the hell not?" I demanded, my voice raising in volume. The rejection felt like a slap in the face after everything we had been through.

"Karl," Sergeant Claiborne finally looked up at us, his expression stern. "We already have other patrols scheduled to pass by her house regularly. If she returns home, we'll catch her and bring her in for questioning."

The rational part of my brain understood his logic, but the rest of me was too caught up in the moment, too invested in the chase. "For fuck's sake!" I exploded, storming out of his office.

Sarah hurried after me as I made my way to the carpark. "Karl, wait! Where are you going?" she asked, her voice laced with concern.

"To find Gladys," I replied curtly. My mind was made up; I couldn't just sit back and wait.

"Karl. Don't," she cautioned. "The Sergeant denied the request. You can't."

Her warning fell on deaf ears. "I don't really care what the Sergeant said," I snapped back, the day's pent-up frustration finally erupting. I got into the car and slammed the door, my breathing heavy, my mind a whirlwind of emotion and confusion. *What the fuck is wrong with me?* I silently questioned myself, my thoughts spiralling. *Hearing voices, seeing things, jumping at shadows...* "I must be losing my fucking mind," I muttered to myself, the words bitter and filled with self-reproach.

Suddenly, Sarah was there beside me, startling me as she jumped into the passenger seat. "I'm coming with you," she declared firmly.

Her determination, her refusal to leave me to face this alone, was both surprising and grounding. In that moment, I realised how much I relied on her, not just as a partner in the field, but as a grounding force in the midst of chaos. Her presence was a reminder that, no matter how deep into the rabbit hole I felt I was falling, I wasn't alone.

In a moment that blurred the lines between gratitude and frustration, I found myself acting on an impulse I didn't fully understand. I leaned over and kissed Sarah firmly on the lips. To my surprise, she kissed me back. It was a brief, intense moment that felt like a small reprieve from the chaos of our day. I pulled away, the silence between us heavy with unspoken thoughts, and started the ignition. Out of the corner of my eye, I saw Sarah smiling, a subtle gesture that offered a fleeting sense of peace. *Maybe she will forgive me*, I thought, a glimmer of hope amidst the storm of emotions swirling inside me.

We drove in silence, the atmosphere in the car charged with the intensity of our shared experiences. As we headed down the Brooker towards Gladys' house, my mind was a whirlwind. Images of Sarah, Gladys, and Beatrix flickered through my thoughts, each evoking different emotions, different connections. The boundaries between reality and my thoughts blurred as their smiling, laughing faces haunted my mind. I closed my eyes for a split second, trying to clear the overwhelming rush of images.

"Shit Karl!" Sarah's voice cut through my reverie, sharp with alarm. I had drifted into the left lane, narrowly avoiding a collision with another vehicle. Reacting instinctively, I jerked the wheel back, regaining control of our lane. My head throbbed with a growing ache, the mental images continuing their relentless parade across my consciousness.

The tensions pulsing from my head began to spread throughout my body. I shifted uncomfortably in my seat, when the first pulse of tension reached my groin and ran along my dick.

Sarah's voice brought me back to the present. "Where are we going?" she asked, her tone a mixture of concern and confusion as I unexpectedly exited the highway

I couldn't bring myself to answer her. I was acting on an instinct I didn't fully understand, driving us towards the Entertainment Centre, which lay in darkness. *There would be no events tonight,* I thought to myself. *At least not any that would be watched.* Pulling into the empty, dimly lit parking lot, I chose a spot at the far end, away from any potential prying eyes.

"What are you doing?" Sarah's voice was laced with confusion and a hint of panic as she faced me, her youthful brow creased with worry.

In a moment of misguided impulse, I leaned in to kiss her again. But my movement was abruptly halted by the seatbelt, which jammed and tightened, stopping me mere inches from her face. Frustrated, I tugged at the belt, but it only seemed to constrict further. "Ah shit," I muttered, my teeth clenched in irritation.

Sarah's gaze was intense, her eyes searching mine. Without warning, she pushed me back against the seat with surprising force. The seatbelt snapped back, tightening its grip, effectively pinning me to my seat.

Confusion and shock washed over me. *Had I misread the situation so completely? I thought there was something between us, a connection that went beyond partnership.* My body reacted to her nearness, but the choke in my throat stifled any words of apology I might have uttered.

As I heard the click of Sarah's seatbelt unfastening, I made a futile attempt to lean forward, hindered by my own seatbelt. Desperately, I reached out to stop her from leaving, but she pushed me back once more. Tears welled in my eyes, one escaping down my cheek, a physical manifestation of my internal turmoil.

Sarah faced me, shoving her hands into my chest. I saw the raging wildfire in her eyes. Unexpectedly, she pressed her lips against mine. Feeling her tongue run the length of my rough lips, I opened my mouth and allowed her tongue to find mine.

I couldn't believe the passion I was feeling. *Is this love?* As we kissed, I reached out my left hand and held her firmly behind her neck, drawing her in closer to my body.

With surprising force, Sarah's hands ripped open my still-damp shirt, sending several buttons scattering around us, her hands cool against my warm chest. Moving her hand along my inner thigh, Sarah rubbed with the tips of her fingers, several times, before making her way further along to find the centre of my passion.

I gripped her waist, sliding my hands under her shirt and gradually up her smooth, toned stomach. Sarah's breasts rested comfortably in my large hands as I massaged them gently, causing moans of pleasure to escape Sarah's lips as we continued kissing.

As Sarah unbuckled my seatbelt my cock pulsed with such energised force I thought it would burst. Unzipping my trousers, I moaned as she took me in her mouth, her cool hands, soft against my firm dick, sending pulses of electrifying intensity with every movement she made.

She came up to kiss me again, with an intensity I had never experienced before. I pulled her trousers down to her ankles and steadied her clumsily as she climbed onto my lap.

Sliding my seat back as far as it would go, it stopped with a harsh thud. The car rocked to the rhythm of our energetic lovemaking.

❖

Sarah fell back into her own seat, exhausted. "Still want to go and see Gladys?" she asked with a wide, cheeky smile.

"No," I replied bluntly, my eyes closed as I contemplated our next move. The unresolved questions about Gladys were frustrating, but another idea was taking shape in my mind. "I think it's time to pay Beatrix a visit."

"Beatrix?" Sarah echoed in surprise. "Who the fuck is Beatrix?"

"Beatrix Cramer. Gladys' sister," I explained, feigning a nonchalance I didn't feel. "I've done my homework," I lied. The truth was, I didn't need to look up Beatrix in any database. My past encounters with her were etched deeply in my memory.

"What, right now?" Sarah's expression was a mix of confusion and incredulity.

"Yes," I said firmly, reaching into the back seat for a small duffel bag. I pulled out a fresh grey t-shirt and quickly changed. "And I need to go alone."

Sarah sat motionless, her eyes wide with a mixture of anger and disbelief. Ignoring her gaze, I stretched across her, struggling to reach the door handle. My attempt to open her door was only partially successful. It opened slightly before swinging shut again, but my message was clear.

Sarah collected her belongings, her movements sharp and decisive. She opened the door and stepped out into the night. "You can be such a prick sometimes Karl," she said, her voice harsh with emotion before slamming the door.

I sat there for a moment, trying to make sense of my own actions. *Am I making the right decision?* The unease in my gut said otherwise, but I couldn't turn back now. I watched in the rearview mirror as Sarah dressed herself in the dark, the reflection tinged with regret. *She'll be okay*, I reassured myself. *Her house is less than a ten-minute walk away.*

With a heavy heart, I pulled out of the car park and turned onto the highway. The road stretched out before me, a path leading towards an uncertain encounter with Beatrix. My mind was a storm of thoughts and emotions, each as tumultuous as the weather we had already experienced. But there was no turning back now. I was committed to this course of action, for better or worse.

❖

As I pulled up outside the Cramer residence, a wave of anxiety washed over me. The house was modest, unassuming, but it was charged with the weight of my past interactions with Beatrix's family. The last time I had spoken to Brett and Wendy Cramer was during the investigation into the death of Beatrix's partner, an event that had driven a deep wedge between us. Their directive had been clear and unyielding: I was not welcome here. Two years of silence had passed, but would that be enough to soften their stance?

With trepidation, I approached the front door, my knocks almost timid. I had barely tapped the door, surprised when it actually swung open.

"Fuck off, Karl," Wendy snapped, her voice harsh and unwelcoming. She moved to close the door almost as soon as she had opened it.

"Wendy, wait!" I called out instinctively, my hand shooting out to stop the door just inches from closing on my face. I gently pushed against the door, but Wendy countered with a firm resistance.

"You don't get to call me Wendy," she retorted, her voice laced with bitterness.

I felt a pang of regret, the memory of our last encounter and its unpleasant aftermath vivid in my mind. "Mrs Cramer, please. I need to speak with Beatrix," I pleaded, my voice desperate. "It's urgent."

There was a momentary pause, a slight easing of the pressure on the door. "She's not home," Wendy stated firmly.

But then, catching me off guard, Mrs Cramer gave the door a final, decisive shove. I stood there, a mixture of frustration and defeat washing over me as the door clicked shut in front of me. My lead, my hope of finding answers with Beatrix, seemed to evaporate with that closed door.

I took a moment, standing there on the Cramers' doorstep, collecting my thoughts. The day had been a series of dead ends and emotional turmoil. I felt drained, my mind reeling from the events and the many unanswered questions that lingered. *What now?* The question echoed in my mind as I turned away from the door, contemplating my next move. The investigation was far from over, but each step seemed to lead only to more complexity and uncertainty.

❖

Returning home to Jargus was the one piece of normalcy in a day that had been anything but. His cheerful wag and excited greetings were a balm to the tumult of the day. "I'm sorry, Jargus," I said softly, crouching down to his level for a few slobbery, welcome kisses. "I haven't been around for you much lately, have I?" I asked, though I knew I wouldn't get an answer. His presence was a quiet reassurance, a reminder of simpler joys.

I headed straight for the shower, letting the hot water wash over me, rinsing away the day's sweat and stress. The water felt refreshing, a small oasis of calm in the storm of my thoughts. As the steam filled the room, the bathroom door creaked open. Instinctively, my eyes snapped open, and adrenaline surged through me, ready for whatever threat might be looming.

"Shit, Jargus!" I exclaimed with relief and a little laughter. "You almost gave me a heart attack!" There he was, sitting just outside the shower, a clean towel held in his mouth. His impatience for bedtime was both endearing and amusing.

With a renewed appreciation for Jargus's simple, unwavering companionship, I hastened through my nighttime routine. In bed, Jargus snuggled up against me, his warmth and presence a comforting anchor. Propped up with pillows, I attempted to do some last-minute research on my phone. My goal was to look up Killerton Enterprises, but the day's exhaustion was overwhelming. My eyes blurred, struggling to focus on the screen. The search term "Killerton Ent—" was as far as I got before my eyelids grew heavy, and I slid down into the comfort of my king-size bed, surrendering to sleep.

4338.212

(31 July 2018)

A DEADLY AFFAIR

4338.212.1

In the silent darkness of my car, I found myself parked outside the house of Luke Smith and Jamie Greyson, my gaze fixated on the building. The cool breeze flowed through the open window, brushing gently against my face, a stark contrast to the tension knotting inside me. Three long hours had passed with no sign of movement from the house, the wait stretching on interminably.

Then, suddenly, a lamp flickered to life in a second-story window, casting a soft orange glow that spilled into the night. My arms tingled with a rush of excitement. Leaning out of the car window, I rubbed my eyes, questioning the reality of what I was seeing. *Is someone finally home?* My heart pounded with anticipation, the implications of this moment racing through my mind. *What would I do if I came face to face with Luke Smith?*

As I watched, a shadow moved behind the bedroom blinds – a woman's silhouette. *Could it be Gladys?* I was transfixed as the blinds opened, revealing the figure in full view. It was her – Gladys. She leaned out the window, giggling into the darkness, seemingly carefree.

Then a man appeared behind her. My initial reaction was fear for Gladys. *Was she aware of his presence?* I shifted in my seat, kneeling to get a better view. I felt an urge to warn her, but as I watched, the man wrapped his arms around her from behind, holding her close. Her light giggle reached my ears on the wind. The man leaned in, kissing her gently on the neck, the intimacy of their actions unmistakable. It had to be

Luke. Luke and Gladys, entwined in what seemed to be an affair.

A surge of triumph welled up inside me. *It all makes sense now!* The pieces of the puzzle seemed to fall into place, the affair explaining so much of the mystery and secrecy surrounding these individuals.

But my fleeting moment of joy was quickly overshadowed by a creeping sense of foreboding. It filled the car, emanating from the open window, a palpable presence that dampened my initial elation.

I watched the seemingly happy couple. Gladys's expression of passion quickly turned to surprise and then pain, as I saw, in that instant, Luke drive a small knife he had been concealing, right up to the hilt, into her abdomen. Gladys's anguished scream echoed through the car. I reached for my throat, clawing at the foreboding that held my voice captive.

Luke's knife ripped a gash across her belly as I watched, helpless. Gladys's intestines unravelled as they flopped out of her and onto the ground below. The screaming stopped. Blood dripped below as more organs fell from the gaping hole. When the last drop of blood fell, Luke threw the lifeless body from the window. It plummeted to the ground, landing with a sickening thud.

As I clambered out of the car, my movements were clumsy and hurried, driven by a mix of adrenaline and shock. I stumbled across the road, my knees scraping painfully against the hard asphalt. It felt like every fibre of my being was focused on the house, on that bedroom window where Luke stood.

Looking up, I caught Luke's gaze. His eyes were like two dark voids, cold and penetrating, sending a chill down my spine. The sight of him standing there, with an evil grin stretching across his face, was unnerving. The small knife he held up only added to the sinister tableau. It glinted ominously in the dim light, a silent but potent threat.

My body reacted with a primal sense of danger; a cold tingle ran through me. And then I heard it - the same voice that had been haunting me, whispering with a chilling, triumphant tone, "Bye Karl."

❖

I woke up abruptly, the remnants of the dream still vivid and unsettling. The sheets beneath me were drenched in sweat, a testament to the intensity of the nightmare that had gripped me. My heart was pounding in my chest, each beat echoing loudly in the silence of the room. The feeling of dread from the dream lingered, a tangible presence in the dark.

As I lay there, trying to catch my breath, a wave of nausea washed over me. The sickness came suddenly, leaving me barely enough time to react. I yanked back the doona in a frantic motion, just as the first convulsive wave of vomit surged up. I was helpless against it, my body reacting violently to the stress and fear that had accumulated over the past days.

The physical reaction was intense, leaving me gasping and disoriented in its aftermath. I lay there for a moment, trying to steady myself, the sour taste in my mouth a bitter reminder of the nightmare's potency. It was more than just a bad dream; it felt like a manifestation of all the tensions, fears, and uncertainties that had been building up inside me.

The image of Luke, his cold gaze and the whispered "Bye Karl," replayed in my mind, sending another shiver down my spine. The dream, though a product of my subconscious, felt ominously real, a twisted reflection of the complexities and dangers of the case I was entangled in.

As I slowly sat up, trying to regain my composure, I knew that this case was taking a toll on me, both physically and mentally. The boundaries between reality and imagination were blurring, and the strain was becoming increasingly apparent.

THE BREAK

4338.212.2

The tension in the car was palpable as Sarah and I drove to our next case, another disappearance that demanded our attention. The silence between us was a heavy blanket, laden with the unspoken words and unresolved issues from last night. Sarah's deliberate avoidance of conversation since my impulsive decision to leave her behind weighed on me. Coupled with the night terror that had jolted me awake in the early hours, my state of mind was far from conducive to any form of conversation, be it casual or profound. I feared any attempt at dialogue might spiral into another heated argument.

As we arrived at our destination, my thoughts momentarily shifted from our strained relationship to the impressive structure before us. The house was adorned with four columns supporting a large balcony, their renaissance-inspired design lending an air of elegance and grandeur to the entrance. "This way please, Detectives," Mrs. Pafistis beckoned, her voice breaking the silence as she welcomed us into her home.

We followed her across the expansive, square marble tiles that led us past a luxurious kitchen. The kitchen boasted stone bench tops and stainless steel appliances, a testament to the affluence that surrounded us. We continued into the main living area, an equally impressive space.

Sarah, perhaps caught off guard by the opulence, couldn't help but express her admiration. "Your house is exquisite," she commented as we entered the room.

"Thank you," Mrs. Pafistis replied with a gracious smile. "Much of this is my husband's handiwork."

"Impressive," Sarah said, and I found myself nodding in agreement. The house was indeed a marvel of design and architecture. Standing there, in the midst of such luxury, my own modest living arrangements seemed even more humble by comparison. It made my small, two-bedroom house feel almost insignificant, a stark contrast to the grandeur before us.

Seated on the Italian leather sofa, the luxurious feel of the material was lost on me as I focused on the task at hand. Mrs. Pafistis sat across from us, her composure calm, belying the gravity of her situation.

Leaning forward, I was eager to commence the interview. "Your full name for the record, please," I requested, notebook and pen ready.

"Sharon Pafistis," she responded, her voice steady.

As I jotted down her name, my handwriting was precise, deliberate. I added the date in the top right corner, ensuring clarity for the records. Looking back up, I took a moment to study Sharon Pafistis. She was thin, with an air of refinement about her. Her features were striking – a pointed, well-shaped nose, large green eyes, and full lips enhanced by perfectly applied nude lipstick. There was an elegance to her appearance that was hard to overlook.

"And you say your husband has gone missing?" I inquired, maintaining a professional demeanour.

"Yes," Sharon nodded, her voice carrying a hint of concern. "Adrian."

"When was the last time you had any contact with him?" I continued, my tone even.

"I last saw him yesterday morning. He said he was going out to meet with a client about a new potential job," she explained, her gaze steady.

A sense of déjà vu crept over me as she spoke. The familiarity of her story struck a chord, echoing the beginnings of Jenny Triffett's case. The similarities were uncanny, almost unsettling. The jitters that I had been struggling with began to resurface, a mix of anxiety and intrigue. It felt as though we were treading familiar ground, yet the circumstances suggested there was more to this than mere coincidence.

"What time was that?" I continued, trying to piece together the timeline.

"I'm not entirely sure. It would have been before nine," Sharon replied, a hint of uncertainty in her voice.

"Have you heard from him since? Any phone calls or text messages?" Sarah chimed in, her movements around the room deliberate and observant.

I glanced over at Sarah, hoping to catch her eye and subtly signal for her to sit back down, but she either missed my cue or chose to ignore it. Her pacing added a layer of intensity to the questioning.

"No, nothing at all," Sharon's response came with a slight falter in her previously composed demeanour, a sign that the gravity of the situation was starting to take its toll.

"Did you know the person he was going to meet with?" I pressed further, my fingers unconsciously crossing for a positive response.

"No, I've never met them before," she admitted, dashing my hopes for an easy lead.

My optimism dwindled, but I persisted. "But you've heard of them?" I asked, looking up from my notebook mid-note, clinging to any thread of connection.

"Yes. I think Adrian had done a few renovation quotes for him before," Sharon offered.

"Is this your husband?" Sarah asked, picking up a small photo frame. It was a candid shot of a couple, smiling blissfully on a sun-kissed beach. My irritation spiked as

Sharon turned her attention to Sarah. Despite my repeated cautions against touching personal items during interviews, Sarah seemed to disregard protocol, especially when it came to photographs. I felt a twinge of frustration, worried that Sharon was on the cusp of revealing a crucial detail.

"Yes, that was taken last year. We were on holiday in Bali. We managed to escape for a week without the kids," Sharon reminisced, a wistful tone in her voice.

"You both look very happy," Sarah observed, throwing a quick glance in my direction.

"Yes, we were," Sharon responded, then quickly corrected herself, "I mean, we are. We've always had a happy marriage."

Sarah, undeterred by my silent pleas for restraint, continued her line of questioning. "You have children then?" she inquired.

"We have two daughters, Sarah and Brooke," Sharon answered, her voice warming with maternal pride.

"Are they home?" Sarah followed up.

"No, they're at my sister's. I didn't want them to be here while I spoke with you," Sharon explained, her gaze shifting slightly.

"We may need to speak with them too," Sarah noted, her tone carrying a hint of caution. Her phone vibrated, breaking the flow of the conversation. "Excuse me a moment," she said, stepping into the adjoining room.

With Sarah momentarily out of the room, I quickly redirected the conversation back to the crucial detail I had been pursuing. "Do you know the name of this client?" I asked Sharon, a sense of urgency underlying my question. I held my breath, waiting for her response, knowing that this could be a pivotal moment in our investigation.

"I think he might have said the client's name was Luke Smith?" Sharon answered, her voice laced with uncertainty.

The mention of Luke Smith sent a jolt through me, tying my stomach in knots. The loud churn of my gut was almost audible, resonating with the implications of her words. The possibility that these disappearances were interconnected suddenly seemed more real, more tangible. A web of connections was forming in my mind, with Luke Smith at its centre.

Suddenly, a loud exclamation from the other room broke the tense atmosphere. "Shit!" Sarah's voice carried clearly, her tone sharp and surprised.

I glanced apologetically at Sharon. "Sorry," I said quickly. We tried to maintain a level of professionalism and refrain from swearing in front of the people we interviewed, but sometimes the circumstances got the better of us.

Sarah walked into the room. "Karl," she said, a look of concern on her face. "You need to come and have a look at this," she said, holding up her phone.

I looked at Sharon again. "Excuse me a moment," I said politely. I got up and made my way over to Sarah then we both stepped back into the adjoining room.

"I've just received the transcripts from Nial Triffett's phone calls," she informed me quickly, her voice laced with a sense of urgency.

"And?" I prompted, eager to understand the connection.

"Ignoring all the missed calls from his wife, check out the last ones," she instructed, handing her smartphone over to me.

I squinted at the tiny font on her screen, reading out the last few names listed, "Steve Lang, Jane, Brian." Then, a name stopped me in my tracks. "This call was from Luke Smith." The significance of the name in this context sent a chill down my spine.

"I know," Sarah confirmed, her expression mirroring the gravity of the situation.

"Fuck, this is bad," I muttered, realising the implications.

"Yeah," Sarah agreed, but she was quick to add more to the unfolding puzzle. "But that–"

Before she could finish, I interjected, connecting the dots aloud. "Sharon was just telling me that she is pretty sure the client who her husband went to see yesterday morning was Luke Smith." The coincidence was too striking to ignore.

Sarah glared at me again. "But that's not all," she said, shoving another image under my nose.

"What's this?" I asked, unsure of what I was looking at.

"It's an image from the security footage of Jamie's bank account withdrawals," she answered.

Studying the image closely, I realised something was off. "Are you sure?" I questioned, bringing the image closer to my face. "But that doesn't look like Jamie."

"It's not," Sarah confirmed, her voice steady. "It's Luke Smith.

"The revelation hit me like a ton of bricks. Luke Smith, a name that had been circling around our investigation, now appeared in the centre of a complex web of connections. His presence in Jamie's bank withdrawal footage added a new, sinister dimension to the case. It was becoming clear that Luke Smith was more than just a peripheral figure; he was intricately involved in a way we had yet to fully understand.

As I processed this new information, the puzzle pieces began to align in a disturbing picture. Luke Smith's involvement in both the Triffett and Pafistis cases, his presence in the bank footage, the phone calls – everything pointed towards a much larger, more complex scheme than we had initially anticipated. The case was unraveling into something far bigger and more intricate than I had imagined, and I couldn't help but feel that we were just scratching the surface.

THE STRUGGLE

4338.212.3

As I stood outside the Sergeant's office, my knuckles rapped sharply against the closed door, a mix of determination and nerves pulsing through me. I had left Sarah behind at Mrs. Pafistis' place, entrusting her to complete the interview. Sharon's revelation about Luke Smith had provided the critical lead I needed, and my focus had shifted entirely to obtaining a warrant for his arrest.

Impatience gnawed at me as I waited for a response from inside the office. *What the hell is taking him so long?* The question echoed in my mind, my frustration mounting with each passing second. I knocked again, harder this time, the sound echoing through the hallway.

Unable to contain my urgency any longer, I turned the handle and pushed the door open, stepping into the Sergeant's office unannounced. The scene that greeted me was one of casual authority: the Sergeant leaned back in his chair, feet propped up on the desk, a picture of relaxed command.

"I'll call you back later to confirm when I'm ready," I overheard him say into the phone, his tone nonchalant. He hung up the phone and looked up at me, his large size-twelve feet still resting comfortably atop each other on the desk.

"Karl, why are you here?" Sergeant Claiborne asked coldly. It was clear that he was not impressed by the intrusion, but I didn't care. There were, I felt, more important matters to be dealt with. Claiborne's dating service could wait. Every week it was a different woman. I knew about it. *Everybody at the station knew about it!* And if they didn't, well, if they were that unobservant, I didn't think they deserved to be in the police force at all.

"I'd like permission to obtain a warrant for the arrest of Luke Smith," I declared, cutting straight to the chase. My voice was firm, reflecting the seriousness of my request.

"On what grounds?" Sergeant Claiborne's question was expected, but I was prepared.

"Four counts of murder," I responded, holding his gaze. My confidence didn't waver, even under his scrutinising look.

"Four?" The Sergeant raised an eyebrow, his interest piqued.

"Yes, Sir," I affirmed. "Luke's partner Jamie Greyson, Jamie's nephew Kain Jeffries, and acquaintances Nial Triffett and Adrian Pafistis."

The Sergeant's skepticism was evident in his response. "Acquaintances? Come on, Karl. You're going to have to do a bit better than that."

I understood his skepticism; the connections weren't typical or straightforward. "We know that Luke made contact with Nial and Adrian, posing as a client and asking to meet up to discuss potential work," I explained, trying to make the connections as clear as possible. "Besides that, I'm not sure what other connection they have," I admitted, my honesty reflecting the gaps in our understanding of the case. *Aside from the fact that Luke is a fucking psychopath.*

Standing before Sergeant Claiborne, I felt the gravity of the situation weighing heavily on me. His skepticism was palpable, and his response was cutting. "Not sure? You think a judge is going to believe 'not sure'?" he questioned with a tone of disparagement.

I tried to defend my position, clutching at the straws of evidence we had. "Nial's phone records show that Luke was the last person he spoke to before he disappeared. We also have footage of Luke making a considerable withdrawal at an ATM from Jamie's bank account," I stated, my voice firm despite the rising doubt.

"A phone call and an ATM withdrawal," the Sergeant echoed my words, his tone unimpressed. "Not exactly arrestable crimes. Has Jamie's bank card been reported missing or stolen?"

His question stopped me in my tracks. I hesitated, realising the gaps in our evidence. "Well, no. But–" I began, only to be cut off.

"No buts, Karl. You know that. If you don't have solid evidence pointing to a crime, then I have no other choice but to deny your request for an arrest warrant."

I felt a sense of desperation creeping in. "Look, I need a search warrant," I said, almost pleading.

"What for?" Sergeant Claiborne asked, his impatience evident.

"Luke Smith's house," I argued, trying to maintain my resolve.

"And what do you expect to find?" he pressed further.

I was at a loss for words. *What do I expect to find?* The question echoed in my mind. All I could envision was the chaos I had created myself – the torn garbage bags and the broken window. "I'm not sure," I admitted, my voice trailing off.

Sergeant Claiborne's gaze bore into me, a mix of pity and disappointment in his eyes. "I think you've answered your request yourself then, haven't you?" he concluded. "Karl, I find your arguments inconclusive and unconvincing, and your evidence is circumstantial at best. Your request is denied, on both grounds."

Defeated and frustrated, I turned to leave the office, my emotions clear on my face.

"Karl," Sergeant called after me, his tone shifting to one of encouragement mixed with caution. "Find Luke, but just don't touch him," he urged.

Storming out of the office, I slammed the door behind me. Overwhelmed with frustration and anger, I hastily sent a text to Detective Lahey.

15:09 Karl: *Claiborne has refused request to obtain either an arrest warrant or search warrant. Glen is on his way to collect you. KJ.*

I was back to square one, but I wasn't going to give up. Luke Smith was still out there, and I knew I had to find him, even if it meant working within the constraints set by the Sergeant. The case was far from over, and I was determined to see it through, no matter the obstacles.

❖

Knowing that Sarah would be more than a little pissed at me for leaving her behind again, I made sure that I left the station before she arrived back. But I had to. My plan for the evening was clear: to stake out Luke's house, to catch him in a criminal act that would justify an immediate arrest. This mission felt personal, a silent vow to bring Luke Smith to justice.

After my usual evening routine and a grateful acceptance of a fresh towel from Jargus, I dressed in the darkest clothes I could find. I filled Jargus' bowl with a few extra dog biscuits as a small apology for leaving him alone, yet again.

The mood that enveloped me was dark and brooding. Dusk was still painting the sky as I parked my car by the river Derwent. I decided to walk up the steep Berriedale Road, thinking it less conspicuous than driving up to Luke's house.

The walk was more exhausting than I had anticipated. Finding a spot among the bushes across the road, I settled down to watch.

The discomfort of my position, the constant shifting every two minutes, began to grate on me. Frustration and impatience bubbled inside as I contemplated abandoning my post and jogging back to the car. But every time I looked up at the house, my resolve hardened.

Visions of what Luke might be doing haunted me – the imagined sight of Gladys' body mutilated and displayed grotesquely in the window fuelled my anger and resolve. The small face peering out from the living room blinds only added to the eerie atmosphere. My thoughts were consumed by the atrocities I believed Luke capable of. He was a monster in my eyes, a threat that needed to be neutralised.

Under the shroud of night, I felt a blend of stealth and foolishness as I checked for any oncoming traffic before darting across the road. Reaching the head-high wooden fence encircling Luke's property, I stood on tiptoe, peering over the top with a focused gaze. The backyard was still, shrouded in darkness with no sign of movement. The house, too, was quiet, no shadows or lights betraying any presence.

A sense of self-doubt crept in. *Is there really any need for this clandestine approach?* Despite this, I couldn't shake off the anger boiling inside me or the thrill of the sneaky operation I had embarked on. I continued my stealthy exploration, skirting along each side of the fence until I reached the top of the driveway.

Standing at Luke's front door, I contemplated knocking. My hand hovered in the air, heart pounding with anticipation. But my past experiences here had taught me that knocking was futile. I needed a different approach, something more direct.

With a sense of trepidation, I pulled out my phone and scrolled through my contacts until I found the name that made my heart skip a beat: Jamie Greyson. It had been years since I last dialled this number, and I wasn't even sure if it was still active. My memories of Jamie, particularly the harrowing one where I had left him to drown, flooded back, intensifying my apprehension.

Taking a deep breath, I tried to steady my nerves. With a sense of inevitability, my finger pressed the call button, but I couldn't bring myself to put the phone to my ear. I wasn't ready to confront the voice of the man I had abandoned all those years ago. Instead, I held the phone before me, staring at the screen, waiting, anticipating. The silence around me was oppressive, filled with the echoes of the past and the weight of the present moment. I stood there, outside Luke's house, torn between the past and the present, caught in a web of emotions and duty.

The faint, yet unmistakable sound of a phone ringing inside the house caught my attention. It was a surreal moment; my call to Jamie's phone was echoing from within the very walls I was surveilling. Was it just a mere coincidence, or something more? Doubts and questions raced through my mind as I leaned closer to the window near the front door, straining to hear better.

The ringing ceased abruptly, replaced by Jamie's voice on the MessageBank, instructing me to leave a message. A chill ran down my spine. *Was Jamie's phone actually inside the house? Could Jamie himself be here?* The possibility sent a surge of both hope and fear through me. *Why hadn't Jamie answered the phone?*

Driven by a mix of curiosity and an urgent need for answers, I redialed Jamie's number, my breath held in anticipation. Once again, the muffled sound of ringing filled the silence inside the house. I moved swiftly to the kitchen window, carefully peeking over the sill to gain a view inside. My heart pounded in my chest as I saw it – Jamie's phone, lying on the kitchen bench, my number flashing on its screen as it rang unanswered.

I stood there, frozen, watching intently for any sign of movement, for anyone to pick up the phone. But the house remained eerily still, no signs of life evident. A nagging thought wormed its way into my mind. *Had someone seen me arrive? Did they know I was here, watching, waiting?*

As I glanced around, ensuring no one was watching, I leaped over the fence into Luke's top-level backyard. Moving with the stealth of a shadow, I stayed low, creeping beneath the bathroom window and skirting the backdoor. I paused when I reached the edge of the back bedroom window, which was veiled in darkness. The blinds fluttered slightly in the night breeze, and I noticed the window was still broken, just as I had left it. A chill ran up my spine, the eerie echo of "Bye Karl" reverberating in my mind. It was a chilling reminder of my night terror, and it stirred a nauseating mix of fear and anxiety within me. My rational mind was screaming at me to leave, but the deep-seated need for answers held me in place.

Positioning myself directly in front of the broken bedroom window, I tightened my black leather gloves and began a meticulous examination of the window's rim. I carefully removed any sharp glass shards that might cut me as I entered, gently placing them on the soft carpet inside. The window was large, almost as wide as the wall, and divided into two sections. As I lifted my right leg through the window, the sensation of the carpet beneath my foot contrasted with the sharp crunch of glass shards.

The situation felt surreal, almost like stepping into another realm. I was breaking into a house to find answers, driven by a sense of justice and a need to stop Luke Smith. The risks were high, but the potential payoff was higher. I was moving beyond the bounds of conventional policing, propelled by a personal vendetta and a professional obligation.

The sudden shout of a man's voice outside caught me off guard, my heart leaping into my throat. In a moment of startled imbalance, I tumbled clumsily into the bedroom, landing amidst the shards of broken glass with a thud. "Shit!" I hissed under my breath, scrambling to press myself against the back wall of the room. My eyes darted frantically, peering through the blinds for the source of the disturbance.

"Hey, it's good to see you again," a young woman's cheerful voice rang out, followed again by the deep, booming voice of the man. It seemed like a casual greeting between neighbours, nothing to do with my clandestine intrusion.

A wave of relief washed over me, though my heart continued to hammer in my chest. I watched the couple for several more minutes as they disappeared into the house across the street. If they had seen me, they appeared not to have paid any attention. It was a small comfort, but I couldn't help feeling exposed and vulnerable.

As I sat in the corner of the nearly empty room, my gaze swept over the space. It was starkly different from before; every single garbage bag was gone. This observation sent a new shiver down my spine. *Were there other bodies hidden here? Was Luke Smith lurking somewhere, waiting for the opportune moment to strike?* The notion of being caught off-guard in such an unarmed position was terrifying.

I slowly stood up, my legs shaky from the adrenaline and the realisation of my precarious situation. Approaching the fully open bedroom door, I felt a slight sense of relief that at least I wouldn't be startled by any creepy voices from behind it tonight. Yet, that small comfort did little to ease the gnawing sense of foolishness coursing through me. I was alone, unarmed, and in the house of a man I believed to be a murderer. It was a stark reminder of the risks I had taken in my quest for justice, and the potential consequences that could follow. With cautious steps, I moved towards the door.

Rooted in place near the toilet that obstructed my view down the hallway, I took a brief pause to collect my thoughts and strategise. I needed a plan, and quickly. My decision was to conduct a swift check of each room on my way to the kitchen, starting with the master bedroom directly opposite me. Peering through the doorway, it seemed all clear, devoid of any immediate threat.

With each step down the long hallway, my tension mounted. A jolt of fear shot through me as I unwittingly caught my own reflection in the bathroom mirror. Shaking off the momentary scare, I refocused on my objective. The entrance to the open-plan kitchen and living room was tantalisingly close now, just a few feet away. I edged forward, taking small, cautious steps.

As I was about to take the final step into the open space, a startling noise halted me: the sound of another body entering through the open window, accompanied by the telltale crackle of glass shards underfoot. My mind whirled with panic and indecision. Confronting the intruder was a risk, especially given my unarmed and vulnerable state. But the area ahead remained shrouded in uncertainty, possibly harbouring unknown dangers.

In that split second, I understood the gravity of my situation. I was trapped between the devil and the deep sea, with no easy escape. The need to make a quick decision pressed heavily on me. *Do I confront the unknown intruder, potentially putting myself in immediate danger? Or do I venture into the unexplored space ahead, where unseen threats might lurk?* Time was not on my side, and the need for swift action was paramount. My heart pounded against my ribcage, adrenaline coursing through my veins as I prepared to make my move, to choose a path in this high-stakes game of cat and mouse.

My instincts surged to the forefront, guiding my actions in the split second I had to decide. The kitchen was just within reach, and I made the snap judgment that it would offer me a chance to arm myself. Without a moment's hesitation, I ducked into the kitchen, bypassing any attempt to survey my surroundings due to the urgency of the situation.

I darted between the island bench and the pantry, heading straight for the corner where I remembered seeing the knife block during our previous visit with Gladys. My heart was racing, each second feeling crucial. Reaching into the darkness where the knife block should have been, my fingers grasped at nothingness. The realisation hit me hard – it was gone. The entire benchtop, usually adorned with utensils and kitchen tools, was eerily empty. "Shit," I muttered under my breath, a mix of frustration and panic setting in. My mind was a whirlwind of emotions, trying to piece together my next move.

In a spur-of-the-moment decision, driven more by instinct than rationale, I snatched Jamie's phone from the island bench. With the phone in hand, I crouched down, concealing myself behind the bench. The tension in the air was palpable as I heard the intruder enter the room. I held my breath, my body tensed for whatever was to come. The sound of footsteps moving about the room filled the silence, each step echoing with the potential of imminent confrontation.

As I stayed hidden, my mind raced with possibilities and scenarios. *Who was this intruder? What were their intentions?* The uncertainty of the situation heightened my senses, and I prepared myself for the possibility of having to defend or reveal myself. The stolen moments of hiding behind the bench felt like an eternity, each second stretching out as I waited for the intruder to make the next move. The adrenaline rush was both a curse and a blessing, sharpening my focus while fuelling my anxiety about the unfolding situation.

As the mysterious presence moved about the room, I remained motionless, holding my breath, expecting an intruder, possibly Luke Smith himself. The tension was almost unbearable.

Then, to my astonishment and slight relief, a cat-sized possum emerged, sniffing its way around the corner of the island bench, its attention drawn to the bin. Realising my presence, startled, the possum scampered away down the hallway. The absurdity of the situation almost made me laugh, but it was tinged with a sense of relief. A small, involuntary smile found its way to my face despite the gravity of the night's events. This was indeed a night to remember – fraught with tension, fear, and now, a touch of unintended comedy.

Just as I was about to stand up, Jamie's phone in my hand suddenly sprang to life, ringing and pulling my thoughts back to the seriousness of the situation. My face hardened as I saw the incoming call. It was Sarah. Confusion clouded my mind. *Why was she calling Jamie's number? What connection did she have to all of this?* Questions swirled in my head, adding to the pile of unanswered mysteries of the night.

I let the phone ring for a few more seconds, my mind racing, trying to make sense of it all. Then, with a mix of curiosity and apprehension, I gingerly pressed the answer button and brought the phone to my ear.

"Hello?" I spoke into the phone, my voice low. I waited, my heart pounding.

Sarah's voice crackled through the phone, her words laced with urgency and fear. "Karl," she said, unmistakably her. "You need to listen to me. You need to get out, right now!"

And then, without warning, the call ended, leaving a silence that was almost deafening.

I stood there, frozen for a moment, bewildered. *How did Sarah know where I was? And why was she so terrified?* A thousand questions raced through my mind, but there was no time to ponder them. I turned towards the living room, my senses heightened, my mind racing.

That's when I saw him – a large man, dressed entirely in black, emerging from the stairs into the room. In the dim light, I couldn't make out his features, but I assumed it had to be Luke. My heart pounded in my chest as adrenaline coursed through my veins.

As the man made a beeline for me, instinct and survival kicked in. I dashed into the dining room, grabbed a dining chair, and swung it in front of me, a desperate attempt to create a barrier between myself and the assailant. But it was futile. The man, with his bearish strength, effortlessly grabbed the top leg of the chair and yanked it from my grip with a single, powerful pull.

I was now defenceless, my only shield torn away. The man's imposing presence loomed over me, his intentions unclear but undoubtedly hostile. My mind raced for a plan, for any means of escape or defence. I was cornered, outmatched in strength, and without a weapon. My training as a detective had prepared me for many scenarios, but the reality of this confrontation was more intense and frightening than any simulation.

I squared my shoulders, ready to face whatever came next. I knew I had to rely on my wits and agility to survive this encounter. The room seemed to close in around us, the tension palpable, a silent battle of wills and strength about to unfold.

My survival instincts kicked into high gear. I knew I had to incapacitate the man, presumed to be Luke, long enough to make my escape. Without a second thought, I charged headfirst, my body a battering ram aimed at his chest. The surprise attack worked. Luke, caught off guard, lost his balance, and we both crashed to the floor in a heap.

Scrambling to my feet, I lunged towards the hallway door, desperate to put distance between us. But my attempt was short-lived. In a swift motion, Luke grabbed my left foot, yanking it out from under me. I hit the floor hard, the carpet grazing my chin as Luke dragged me back.

In a desperate move, I executed a semi-roll, flipping my legs in a kick that sent Luke reeling. The force of my kick was more than I had intended. Luke cried out, losing his grip and his footing on the carpeted stairs. Reacting instinctively, I reached out to stop his fall, my hand finding his in a fleeting moment of connection. But it was too late; Luke's backward tumble had already begun, and in my attempt to save him, I found myself being pulled down the stairs with him.

As Luke and I tumbled down the stairs in a chaotic dance of arms and legs, the adrenaline pumping through my veins numbed me to the immediate pain. My focus was solely on survival, on stopping our fall. But amidst the chaos, my elbow smashed into the wall, dislodging chunks of plaster that rained over us. The pain was a distant sensation, overshadowed by the urgency of the moment.

The end of our tumultuous descent was abrupt and horrifying. By some twist of fate, I found myself landing on Luke's head. The momentum of our fall was relentless, and in a sickening moment, I felt and heard the unmistakable crack of a skull and the snap of a neck, as Luke's head collided with the doorframe, and my legs inadvertently delivered the final, fatal blow.

Staring down at Luke's lifeless body, his dark, unseeing eyes wide open, a profound sense of shock and horror washed over me. I had experienced the harrowing reality of taking a life before, but never like this – never in such a visceral, brutal manner. The raw physicality of it, the close proximity to death, was overwhelming.

Nausea surged within me, bile burning its way up my throat as the reality of what had just happened set in. I had to leave, to escape this scene of accidental death. With a heavy heart and a body trembling from shock, adrenaline, and the aftereffects of the fall, I rolled off Luke's body. I lay on the floor for a moment, giving myself time to process, to allow the nausea to subside.

As I stood up, a sense of urgency and panic took over. I began to pace the downstairs room, my mind racing. "Fuck!" I exclaimed aloud, my pacing intensifying with each step. The reality of the situation was overwhelming – there was a dead man lying in front of me. *What am I going to do with the body?* I couldn't call it in; my presence here was unauthorised, unexplained. I was in deep trouble.

My eyes fell on a small door that led to the cupboard under the stairs. Acting on instinct and desperation, I dragged the heavy body across the floor towards the cupboard. The physical effort was immense, but my mind was too clouded with panic to fully register the strain. As I moved the body, the man's face momentarily caught the edge of the moonlight escaping from behind heavy clouds, and streaming from through the large glass sliding door that led to the backyard. I paused, shifting the face back into the full glow of the moonlight. "Shit," I muttered to myself, a sinking realisation hitting me. *This isn't Luke Smith.*

I didn't recognise the man at all. Frantically, I searched the body for any form of identification, coming up empty except for a small, plastic access card in the man's trouser pocket. It was blank, which struck me as odd, but I didn't have time to ponder its significance. With a heavy heart and a mind clouded with anxiety, I shoved the body into the cupboard under the stairs and forcefully closed the door, listening for the click that confirmed it was shut.

My initial intention of searching the rest of the house for clues linking Luke to the disappearances was now forgotten in the wake of this unforeseen catastrophe. I hastily made my way back up the stairs and, with cautious precision, climbed back out through the broken window.

Once outside, I stuck to the shadows, creeping along the back of the house. I paused for a moment to ensure I was alone before vaulting over the back fence. Then, driven by a mix of fear, guilt, and an overwhelming need to escape, I ran. I ran without stopping, not daring to look back, my mind a whirlwind of thoughts and emotions. The night had taken a turn I never could have anticipated, leaving me with more questions and a deepening sense of dread about the implications of what had just transpired.

❖

The escape back to my car felt like a blur, a frenzied dash fuelled by a mix of exhaustion, emotion, and adrenaline. By the time I reached the river, my breath was ragged, my body aching from the physical and mental toll of the night's events. I let myself into the car, the familiar confines offering a brief respite from the chaos.

Sitting there in the driver's seat, I closed my eyes for a moment, trying to steady my racing heart and calm my jumbled thoughts. The small plastic card I had found on the unknown man's body was still in my hands, turning absentmindedly between my fingers. It felt like a significant clue, yet its meaning was still shrouded in mystery.

With a deep breath, I flicked on the car's interior light, illuminating the cabin with a soft glow. It was time to take a closer look at this enigmatic piece of plastic. As my eyes adjusted to the light, I focused on the card. There was no image, no obvious identifier, but now, under the light, I could see words embossed on its surface.

The words "Killerton Enterprises" were etched into the white plastic, clear and unmistakable. A shiver of apprehension coursed through me as I read the words. Killerton Enterprises – the name was familiar, resonating with an deep sense of dreadful foreboding.

4338.213

(1 August 2018)

THE SCAPEGOAT

4338.213.1

"Detective Jenkins," Sergeant Claiborne called out as I walked by his office door. "A word in my office, please."

As I approached Sergeant Claiborne's office, my steps slowed, a mix of reluctance and apprehension knotting in my stomach. "Detective Jenkins," he called out crisply, his voice slicing through the bustling noise of the station. The mention of my name, coupled with the unexpected summons, set off an alarm in my mind. This was uncharted territory for me, having never been called into the Sergeant's office since earning the stripes of a senior detective. My mind raced, conjuring up every possible reason for this sudden request.

My heart, which had been beating steadily, now thumped erratically against my chest. I paused for a second outside his door, gathering my composure. There was an unwritten rule in our line of work: being called into the Sergeant's office was seldom a harbinger of good news. With each tick of the clock, my anxiety spiked. *Could he know something about last night?* The thought was a jolt of electricity, sending a surge of panic through me. *It was implausible,* I reassured myself. I had already scoured the morning reports with meticulous care. There was no mention of any incidents at the house of Luke Smith and Jamie Greyson, let alone a whisper of a potential homicide.

I bit my lip, hard enough to feel the sting, chastising myself. Leaving the body hidden under the stairs was a reckless move, one that I couldn't afford to ignore for much longer. Yet, there was this nagging feeling, an intuitive whisper, suggesting that the incident might remain undiscovered for now.

Trying to quell the storm of thoughts, I considered more benign possibilities for this meeting. Maybe Sergeant Claiborne simply wanted an update on the current case's progress. It wasn't uncommon for him to seek briefings, albeit usually in a less formal setting. Or perhaps, he had stumbled upon some new piece of information. My mind drifted to the crumpled piece of paper I had lost - Jamie's scrawled note from years ago. At the time, I wasn't too concerned about losing it. The words on that paper were etched in my memory, clear and unyielding. Without context, I had convinced myself, it was just a scrap of paper, meaningless to anyone else.

Taking a deep breath, I squared my shoulders, an attempt to brace myself for whatever lay ahead. I stepped into Sergeant Claiborne's office, a space that felt more like a realm of judgement than a part of the precinct. "Yes, Sergeant. What would you like to see me about?" I asked, my voice steady despite the storm of apprehension swirling inside me.

Sergeant Claiborne, seated behind his desk cluttered with case files and paperwork, looked up at me. His expression was unreadable, a poker face perfected over years of service. "It appears there has been a break-in at Luke Smith's house," he stated, his voice as even as the surface of a still lake.

"A break-in?" I echoed, my mind racing. The words hit me like a shockwave, jolting through my body. "When did that happen?" I managed to ask, trying to mask the sudden surge of panic that threatened to overwhelm me. Inside, a whirlwind of questions raged. *Had Luke found the body? Was he reporting the broken window? But then, why would he?*

Sergeant Claiborne's eyes, sharp and assessing, met mine. "Not sure yet. It was reported very early this morning," he replied, his tone suggesting there was more to the story than he was letting on.

I caught myself just in time, stopping the question that almost slipped out: *really?* My mind was a tumult of confusion and suspicion. I was sure I would have seen any report about this when I checked earlier. *Unless,* a thought whispered treacherously, *someone had requested it be kept off the records. But that made little sense. Why report a break-in and then want it hidden?*

The weight of Sergeant Claiborne's gaze felt like an anvil pressing down on me, his eyes dissecting my every flicker of emotion for signs of guilt or deceit. I struggled to maintain a facade of calm professionalism, but inside, my mind was a whirlwind of chaos and fear. The room seemed to close in around me, the walls inching nearer, as if they were conspiring to trap me in this moment of reckoning. The air was thick, laden with unspoken accusations and the heavy burden of suspicion. I knew I had to navigate this conversation with utmost caution; any misstep could spell disaster.

"I'll grab Detective Lahey and we'll go and check it out immediately," I said quickly, eager to escape the intensity of the room and, more importantly, to steer clear of any further scrutiny that might unveil my deeply buried secret.

"No, Karl," Sergeant Claiborne interjected, his voice firm.

I froze, then turned back to face him, a sense of dread coiling in my stomach. "What do you mean, no?" I asked, my voice laced with a mix of confusion and a creeping sense of alarm.

"The caller wanted to remain anonymous," he explained, his tone measured but unyielding.

I stared at him, my confusion deepening. *What was he implying?* The next words from Sergeant Claiborne struck me like a lightning bolt.

"They said they saw you running from the property late last night," he revealed, his eyes locked onto mine, searching for a reaction.

"What made them think it was me?" I asked, my voice tinged with skepticism. This was absurd. *How could anyone have seen me, let alone identified me?*

Sergeant Claiborne sighed, a sound heavy with regret. "They gave your name, Karl. I have to put you on desk duty until further notice," he said, his voice betraying the reluctance in delivering this verdict.

"What!" I cried out, disbelief and anger coursing through my veins. My mind raced through a list of potential informants, trying to pinpoint who could have betrayed me. "Do you know whether it was a male or female that called it in?" I asked desperately. I was supposed to be the investigator, the one piecing the puzzle together, not the suspect cornered by unforeseen circumstances. The events of the previous night had twisted my role, turning me into a desperate man, eager to keep anyone from discovering the body hidden beneath the stairs.

The Sergeant's frown deepened. "You know I can't tell you that," he said, his voice firm, brooking no argument.

"This is bullshit!" I exclaimed, a mix of frustration and helplessness overwhelming me. Reluctantly, I handed over my gun to the Sergeant, each movement feeling like an admission of guilt, a surrender of my authority and integrity. My badge, once a symbol of pride and responsibility, now felt like a burden too heavy to bear. As I placed my gun into his waiting hand, a part of me couldn't help but wonder if this was the beginning of the end of my career, the unraveling of everything I had worked so hard to build.

❖

The moment I threw my jacket onto the empty seat in the corner of the bullpen, I could feel the weight of every eye in the room on me. The fabric landed with a soft thud, a stark contrast to the turmoil raging inside me. I slumped down at my desk, a fortress of paperwork and cold coffee mugs, feeling a huff of frustration escape my lips. It was a physical manifestation of the storm that was brewing inside.

I've royally screwed myself over this time, I chastised myself silently. The thought echoed in my mind, a relentless reminder of my precarious situation. I knew coming into work today had been a mistake, but I couldn't have predicted it would turn out like this.

My attempts to reach Sarah since last night had been futile, each call going straight to voicemail, each text left unanswered. *It has to be her that called it in*, the thought circled in my head like a vulture. She knew I was at the Smith property; she was the only one who did. But the why of it all eluded me, creating a chasm of confusion and betrayal. *How did she even know I was there? And how, in a twist of fate, did she know to call Jamie's phone, the very phone that I was clutching in my hands at that critical moment?*

The possibility that Sarah might be involved in the disappearances sent a shiver down my spine. It was a thought so chilling, so out of sync with everything I believed, that it made me physically recoil. *We argue constantly*, I reflected, our arguments a strange, twisted dance that, in some bizarre way, I thought brought us closer. But this, this was a betrayal of a magnitude I couldn't fathom. The trust that I thought was the foundation of our relationship, however tumultuous it might be, now seemed like a facade, a house of cards ready to tumble down at the slightest nudge.

I stared blankly at the clutter on my desk, each object a reminder of the normalcy that had been my life until this moment. My thoughts were a whirlpool, sucking me deeper into a vortex of doubt and suspicion. The room around me, usually buzzing with the energy of active cases and clattering keyboards, now seemed distant, as if I were observing it through a fogged lens. I was there, but not quite present, lost in the labyrinth of my own troubled thoughts, trying to piece together a puzzle that seemed to grow more complex by the second.

The bitterness that lingered in my mouth, a physical reminder of my current predicament, was still potent as I answered the desk phone. "Detective Jenkins," I said, trying to sound as composed as possible under the circumstances.

"Detective," a man's voice came through, clear and professional. "This is Detective Jeremy Harding from the Broken Hill Police Station," he introduced himself.

"Broken Hill?" I echoed, my surprise evident in my tone. My eyebrows arched involuntarily. Broken Hill - a name that conjured images of dusty roads and sun-scorched landscapes. "Isn't that the tiny mining town in the middle of nowhere?" I asked, picturing the remote, arid location in my mind.

"It's called the outback," Detective Harding replied with a chuckle, a hint of good-natured ribbing in his voice.

Despite the gravity of my situation, I found myself smiling briefly at his remark. Humour, even in these dire circumstances, seemed to be a universal trait among detectives. "You've got my curiosity piqued. What can I do for you, Detective?" I inquired, genuinely intrigued. *What could possibly link Hobart, a city nestled at the edge of the world, with Broken Hill, one of Australia's oldest mining towns, over a thousand kilometres away near the border of South Australia and New South Wales?*

"I'm investigating the disappearance of a young man who is believed to have travelled from Broken Hill over a week ago after getting into an argument with his wife, and he has not been heard from since," Detective Harding began.

"According to our investigation, we understand his brother bought him a plane ticket to fly from Adelaide to Hobart. Security footage has confirmed that Paul boarded the flight, but we've been unable to contact the brother," he explained.

I sighed silently, my gaze drifting to the mounds of paperwork that adorned my desk. Each file, each document, represented a unique tangle of mysteries and human drama. It felt almost overwhelming. *What's the deal with all these missing men lately?* The thought churned in my mind, a constant reminder of the grim reality of my profession. Another case, another missing person - it was beginning to feel like a relentless tide, each wave crashing over me just as I managed to catch my breath.

"And what is the brother's name?" I asked into the phone, pen poised over a notepad, ready to scribble down any pertinent details. Despite the chaos swirling around my own situation, the detective in me couldn't help but latch onto a new puzzle, a welcome albeit temporary diversion from my own troubles.

"Luke," the voice on the other end replied, a tone of experience in his voice. "Luke Smith."

"Luke Smith?" I echoed, my hand freezing mid-sentence. The name echoed in my head, reverberating like a bell tolling a grim portent.

"Yes. That's correct," the detective confirmed.

"Shit!" The exclamation slipped out before I could catch it, a visceral response to the connection that was rapidly forming in my mind.

"You know him then?" Detective Harding's voice crackled with curiosity through the phone.

I rubbed my forehead, feeling a headache beginning to form, the edges of concern gnawing at my thoughts. *How many bodies would we find at the end of all of this?* The question haunted me, a spectre lurking in the recesses of my mind.

"Yeah," I finally responded, my voice a mix of resignation and grim determination. "We've been investigating him for the last week. We suspect he is responsible for the disappearance of at least five other people. I wasn't aware that his brother was in the state."

"We were hoping you might be able to check and confirm for us where Paul went after leaving the Hobart airport. Assuming he actually left the airport," Detective Harding said, a hint of hope in his tone.

"Sure," I agreed, feeling the familiar surge of determination that always came with a new lead. The detective part of me, honed over years of experience, automatically kicked into gear, offering a brief respite from the personal turmoil that threatened to consume me. "Email me through the flight details and I'll look into it straight away." My hand moved almost of its own accord, scribbling a note on the pad in front of me. The simple, mundane act of writing felt strangely comforting, like a lifeline anchoring me in the midst of a storm of spiralling thoughts.

"The rest of Luke's family live in Adelaide. Do you think they might be in danger?" Detective Harding's question pierced through the phone, bringing a new dimension to the case that I hadn't fully considered.

"Hmm," I mused aloud, buying a moment to gather my thoughts. "We're monitoring all airports and ports out of Tasmania. I think it's unlikely he'd slip past and make it to the mainland. But I'll let you know the moment I find anything," I promised, even as a nagging sense of unease started to settle in my stomach. The possibility of Luke's family being in danger added another layer of urgency to an already complicated situation.

"Thank you, Detective Jenkins," Harding said, his voice conveying a sense of gratitude mixed with the shared burden of responsibility that all detectives carry. Then he hung up the phone.

In a moment of frustration, I threw a pen at the wall in front of me, watching as it clattered against the surface and fell to the floor. The sound echoed in the quiet of the office, a stark reminder of my growing agitation. I'd been so laser-focused on Jamie and the intricacies of his disappearance that I hadn't even considered reaching out to Luke's family. It was an oversight, a rookie error that gnawed at me. I should have known better. Maybe the Sergeant was right, maybe I was too close to this case, too entangled in its web to see the bigger picture.

I leaned back in my chair, feeling the weight of every decision, every missed opportunity pressing down on me. The realisation that I might be losing my grip on the case was a bitter pill to swallow. I had always prided myself on my ability to stay detached, to view each case with a clear, objective eye. But this time, it felt different. The lines were blurring, and I was caught in the middle, struggling to find my footing.

The dark screen of my phone suddenly lit up, piercing the gloom of my office. A new message popped up, a beacon of potential in the midst of my growing despair. My eyes immediately focused on the text, a surge of adrenaline coursing through me. It was from one of the junior officers I had assigned to monitor the airport for any sign of Luke, Jamie, or Kain. Their diligence in this task was one of the few things I could rely on in this ever-twisting case.

Officer: *Detective Jenkins - Luke caught first flight from Hobart this morning, bound for Adelaide. Flight would have landed by now.*

This is perfect, I thought, a plan rapidly forming in my mind. *If I play my cards right, I may just be able to pin last night's... accident... on Luke.* The logic was clear and cold in my head. If the information was accurate, Luke's hasty departure from the state, especially so early in the morning, would cast a heavy shadow of guilt over him. I was growing more certain by the minute that this wouldn't be the only body we'd find connected to him.

With a sense of urgency, I dialled the Adelaide CIB, my voice steady as I relayed the information. I made sure to emphasise that we had just received intel about Luke Smith, suspected of being behind the disappearance of at least half a dozen people, including his partner and brother. He had landed in Adelaide earlier today. I suggested, with a sense of grim necessity, that they send a patrol to Luke Smith's parents' house immediately. If Luke was indeed in the throes of a psychotic breakdown, I argued, then the rest of his family could be in serious danger.

Once the call ended, I slumped back into my chair, a sense of emptiness washing over me. I had expected to feel a sense of relief, perhaps even satisfaction, in steering the suspicion towards Luke, thereby diverting attention from my own actions. But instead, a heavy wave of nausea and paranoia hit me. The screen of my computer stared back at me, its blackness mirroring the dark turn my thoughts had taken. Planting the seeds of suspicion against Luke had not eased my conscience; it had only added to the turmoil. My head felt like it was sinking below the surface, drowning in a sea of sickness and guilt, as my stomach churned with the realisation of what I had just set in motion.

THE ARREST

4338.213.2

"Detective Karl Jenkins," I announced into my mobile, trying to infuse a sense of control and calm into my voice that I wasn't really feeling.

"Detective," came a young woman's voice, tinged with an unmistakable strain of anxiety and fear.

I recognised Jenny Triffett's voice immediately. It had a certain firmness to it, a strength born of adversity, yet there was an underlying soothing quality, like a calm surface hiding turbulent depths.

"Mrs. Triffett," I responded, shifting in my seat to a more attentive posture. "What can I do for you?"

"I want to know what's going on with the investigation into my missing husband," she demanded, her voice carrying a mix of desperation and resolve.

"Have you not heard anything further from him?" I inquired, my tone gentle. "No calls. No text messages?"

"Nothing!" Jenny's response was sharp, a snap of words that spoke volumes of her frustration and fear.

"We're still investigating several new leads," I assured her, trying to sound confident, to provide her with a semblance of hope in the midst of her turmoil.

Then, a soft sob broke through the line, pulling at my heartstrings. "Please, Karl," Jenny's voice, now breaking with emotion, pleaded. "Just tell me something, anything!" she begged.

I paused for a moment, my mind momentarily distracted. My eyes wandered towards the other end of the office. There,

I saw Gladys Cramer, escorted by Sarah, passing by the door. *They must be heading to an interview room,* I thought, a surge of curiosity mingling with my concern. *How did Sarah manage to bring Gladys in? What new development had I missed?*

"Are you still there, Detective?" Jenny's voice, laced with a growing worry, jolted me back from my thoughts.

"Ahh... yeah... Look Jenny, I'm really sorry. I'll call you back in a couple of hours," I replied, my voice trailing off. I hung up the phone hastily, cutting off the call before Jenny had the chance to respond. The urgency to find out what Sarah and Gladys were up to gnawed at me, overriding my conversation with Jenny. I couldn't afford to lose track of any development in this convoluted case, especially not now when every piece of information could be a crucial lead. As I hung up, a mixture of guilt and necessity battled within me, but the detective's instinct in me knew where my immediate priorities lay.

❖

"And where do you think you're going?" Sergeant Claiborne's voice rang out, halting me in my tracks as I jogged down the corridor. I glanced ahead and saw Sarah ushering Gladys into the interview room at the far end. The urgency to know what was happening was almost overwhelming.

"Fuck it," I muttered under my breath, my pace slowing to a hesitant walk. A sense of defeat washed over me as the interview room door closed with a soft, definitive click - a barrier now standing between me and whatever crucial conversation was unfolding inside.

Sergeant Claiborne's presence loomed behind me, his shadow stretching long and imposing on the floor. It was a physical reminder of his authority, and my current precarious standing.

I turned, intending to bypass him, to escape further scrutiny. As I moved, I carefully avoided making eye contact, a futile attempt to shield myself from the Sergeant's penetrating gaze.

"Karl," he said, his voice carrying a weight of seriousness that caused me to pause. It wasn't just the authority in his tone, but something else - a hint of concern, perhaps, or warning.

I halted, standing still as Sergeant Claiborne brushed past me. His proximity was a silent assertion of control, a reminder of the hierarchy within the precinct.

"Follow me," he instructed, his back already to me as he walked away. He didn't turn around, didn't wait to see if I complied. It was an order, not a request.

Reluctantly, I followed, my footsteps echoing hesitantly in the hallway. Standing in the doorway of his office, I was gripped by a sudden reluctance to enter. The threshold felt like a line between the known and the unknown, and I wasn't sure I was ready to cross it. The possibility of what the Sergeant might say filled me with a sense of dread. Being called into his office twice in one day - it was unprecedented, and my mind raced with all the potential bad news that could be awaiting me. The walls of the corridor seemed to close in around me, the air heavy with unspoken tension and the weight of impending revelations.

"I'm about to read Sarah's report from this morning," Sergeant Claiborne announced, his voice steady and purposeful. He held a manilla folder, the contents of which were unknown to me but carried an air of significance. With a casual yet deliberate motion, he tossed it onto the uncluttered surface of his desk, the folder landing with a soft thud that seemed to resonate through the room.

The adrenaline already coursing through my veins spiked at his words. Instinctively, my eyes darted toward the door, ensuring it remained open. My mind, trained for quick thinking and rapid response, was already running through multiple escape scenarios, each plan unfolding in tandem with the others, ready for deployment should the need to flee arise.

"Oh," was the only response I could muster. The word came out feeble, even to my own ears, but I was too preoccupied with the potential implications of Sarah's report to articulate anything more substantial. I feared that any attempt to speak further would betray me, revealing the anxiety that was threatening to overwhelm my carefully maintained composure.

Sergeant Claiborne moved slowly, almost methodically, as he unlocked his top drawer and reached inside. "You can have your gun back now, Karl," he said, his tone neutral as he handed the weapon over to me.

I accepted the gun, the familiar weight of it in my hand bringing a small measure of comfort. "Thank you, Sergeant," I replied, securing it back in its holster. The simple action felt like a restoration of a part of my identity, a piece of myself that had been temporarily stripped away.

For a moment, we just continued to stare at each other, an unspoken conversation hanging in the air between us. I could sense there was something more, something the Sergeant wasn't saying. It was there, hidden in the depths of his eyes, a hint of knowledge or concern that went beyond the mere details of the visit to Luke's house this morning.

"That's all," Sergeant Claiborne finally said, breaking the silence. He gestured towards the door, a clear dismissal. "And close the door behind you," he added, his voice carrying the finality of a chapter closing.

As I turned to leave, a swirl of emotions and thoughts tangled within me. Relief at having my gun returned, confusion over the unread contents of Sarah's report, and a lingering sense of unease about what remained unsaid. The click of the door closing behind me felt like a punctuation mark, leaving me to ponder the mysteries still unsolved and the paths yet to be taken.

❖

I slumped back into my chair, feeling the full weight of the day's events pressing down on me. The seat, once a place of focus and determination, now felt like a holding cell, confining me in a limbo of uncertainty and anxiety. I had waited half the day, each minute stretching out endlessly, for the all-clear to go back into the field, back to the environment where I felt most in control, where I could actively chase down leads and make a difference.

The apprehension gnawing at me was relentless. Not knowing who had called in the report or what they might uncover at the scene was like a slow poison, eating away at the remnants of my sanity. Each tick of the clock seemed to echo in the otherwise silent room, a constant reminder of the unresolved mysteries hanging over me.

Now that I had my gun back, a symbol of my reinstated authority and purpose, I found myself still anchored to my desk, waiting. Waiting for Sarah to return from her interview with Gladys. Waiting for some piece of information that could either salvage the situation or send it spiralling further out of control. The suspense was like a physical entity, a heavy cloud looming over me, draining the energy from my body.

I found myself staring blankly at the computer screen, the pixels blurring into an indistinct haze. My mind was a carousel of thoughts and theories, each spinning around with no clear resolution in sight. The office, usually a buzzing hive of activity and purpose, now seemed eerily quiet, as if reflecting my internal turmoil.

Every so often, I'd glance towards the door, anticipating Sarah's return, each time met with disappointment as the doorway remained empty. The waiting was the hardest part – the not knowing, the helplessness of being stuck in a state of inaction. I tapped my fingers on the desk, a restless rhythm that mirrored my inner restlessness, feeling a mix of eagerness and dread for what Sarah's report might reveal. The pieces of the puzzle were out there, but for now, they remained just out of reach, hidden in the shadows of unfolding events.

❖

After what felt like an eternity of waiting, the familiar sound of Sarah's footsteps finally approached. I glanced up as she returned to her desk. Her presence, normally a source of camaraderie and support, now felt like another element in the complex puzzle I was desperately trying to solve.

"I see you got your gun back," she commented casually, her eyes briefly flicking towards the holster at my side.

I didn't reply. Instead, I fixed her with a look that I hoped conveyed my need for answers, my demand for an explanation about what had transpired in her absence.

"They didn't find anything," she began, her voice betraying a hint of uncertainty. "Nobody answered the door, and the premise was all secured," she continued.

I was puzzled by this turn of events. "So, you didn't go inside?" I asked, trying to piece together the situation in my mind.

"No," Sarah replied. She settled into her chair, the familiar sound of the wheels rolling over the floor as she pulled herself toward her desk. Then she looked directly at me, a seriousness in her gaze. "Oh," she added, "And the broken window has been fixed," she said, her eyes scrutinising my face for any hint of a reaction.

I felt a jolt of surprise, my mind racing to process this new information. My immediate instinct was defensive. "Are you spying on me?" I blurted out, the words leaving my mouth before I could weigh their implications.

Sarah's face drained of colour. "No," she said defensively, her body language shifting as she turned back to her computer, creating a physical barrier between us.

"Sarah," I said, my voice softer this time. I didn't like the tension that had crept into our interaction, the strain that was palpable in the air between us.

"I have a report to finish," she replied, her tone icy, a stark contrast to the warmth that usually characterised our exchanges.

I let several minutes pass, the silence between us thick with unspoken words and emotions. I needed to bridge the gap, to restore some semblance of normalcy to our relationship. "Sarah," I said again, my voice barely above a whisper. She didn't look up, her attention seemingly fixed on her computer screen. "Luke arrived in Adelaide this morning," I informed her, hoping this piece of information would somehow mend the rift that had formed, unaware of how she would receive it or what her reaction might be.

❖

Exhausted and weary, both mentally and physically, from a day that seemed to consist of nothing but clashes with Sarah and the elusive pursuit of Luke Smith, I was on the verge of leaving the station. Just as I began to gather my things, the shrill ring of the desk phone pierced the silence of the nearing end of the day.

"Ah, shit," I muttered under my breath, casting a glance over to Sarah's desk. She, too, appeared to be winding down, preparing to leave the station for the night. The phone's insistent ringing pulled my attention back, its sound almost accusatory in the quiet of the evening.

I noted the interstate number flashing on the caller ID as I picked up the handset. "Detective Jenkins," I said, my voice betraying a hint of the day's weariness.

For the next few minutes, my role in the conversation was mostly that of a listener. The information coming through the other end of the line was concerning, each word adding weight to an already heavy burden. My brow furrowed deeper with each passing second, the creases a testament to the gravity of what I was hearing. The situation, it seemed, was not just unresolved but actively worsening.

"Thank you for the update. Good night to you too, sir," I said eventually, my tone more formal than I intended, a reflex of professionalism in a moment of personal turmoil. I ended the call abruptly, not out of rudeness, but out of a need to process the new information, to absorb its implications in solitude.

The phone clicked softly as I returned it to its cradle, the weight of the call still pressing heavily on my mind. A sense of foreboding, thick and ominous, settled over me like a dense fog. The puzzle pieces of the case were in motion, shifting and turning in ways that were elusive and perplexing. I stood there, momentarily transfixed, my hand still lingering on the phone, my thoughts racing to make sense of the new information. The precinct, usually buzzing with activity, now lay quiet, its silence amplifying the echo of the day's events. It felt surreal, like a theatre after the final act, when the audience has left and only the ghost of the performance remains.

"Well, you look grim," Sarah's voice suddenly cut through my reverie. I hadn't noticed her approach; she had silently manoeuvred herself to my side, likely in an attempt to eavesdrop on my conversation. Her presence, once a source of camaraderie, now felt like an intrusion into my troubled thoughts.

"Who was it?" she asked, her curiosity evident.

I couldn't help but respond with a touch of petulance, "I thought you weren't talking to me," reflecting the childishness that sometimes surfaced in our strained exchanges.

Sarah frowned, clearly torn between maintaining the cold war of silence we had been waging and her inherent drive to solve crimes. It was a battle I knew all too well, the detective in her always striving to rise above personal conflicts.

"Just tell me," she said bluntly, her professional curiosity overriding any residual animosity.

My expression grew even more serious, if that was possible. "That was Detective Santos from the Adelaide CIB," I divulged, feeling the weight of each word. "They called to provide a courtesy update."

Sarah's gaze was intense, expectant, urging me to continue. She gestured with a subtle movement of her hand, silently prompting me to give her more details.

"There's not much to say, really," I began, feeling a sense of futility as I recounted the scant information. "When they arrived at Luke's parent's house, there was nobody there. They have an officer watching the property, but there has been no sign of anybody. Both of the family cars are still at the house. There's no sign of forced entry." I paused, collecting my thoughts. "They questioned the neighbours to see if they had seen anything suspicious."

"And?" Sarah prodded further, her eyes keen and expectant. She was like a dog with a bone when it came to getting information, and I knew she wouldn't let it go easily.

"Well–" I began, trying to articulate the only piece of information that had felt even slightly significant in the call. "The only piece of information that seemed remotely useful was that the elderly lady across the street said she saw a young man, matching Luke's description, arrive at the house some time before lunch. She didn't see or hear anything unusual and hadn't noticed anybody leave the house all day."

"Well, that's great," Sarah chimed in, her tone trying to infuse some optimism into the grim narrative.

I shook my head, not entirely convinced by her attempt to lift my spirits. "Well, not really. All it implies is that Luke really is in Adelaide and maybe went to his parent's house. Anything beyond that is circumstantial."

"But?" Sarah pressed, her intuition clearly picking up on something I hadn't said.

"What do you mean 'but'?" I responded, a bit thrown off by her perceptiveness.

"I see a 'but' on your face. You should know you can't hide your suspicions from me by now," she said, her confidence piercing through the heaviness of the conversation, a faint glimmer of our usual playful banter returning.

I managed a slight smile amidst a heavy sigh. "But it doesn't make any sense," I admitted. "They did a thorough search of the property and all they found was a single drop of fresh blood on the shed door."

"Fresh?" Sarah's tone perked up, a spark of enthusiasm in her voice.

"Apparently, it was still wet. They've taken a sample and sent it to the lab for priority testing. In the meantime, they're having forensics spend the next forty-eight hours examining the house and property for traces of human remains. Or anything, really," I explained, feeling a mix of hope and skepticism at the potential outcomes.

"That is very bizarre," Sarah agreed, her brow furrowing in thought.

I nodded in agreement. "Whatever Luke is up to, he's been very precise so far. We just need something, anything, that will give us some answers." I paused, a sense of realism creeping into my voice. "Knowing our luck, I don't expect forensics will turn up anything new. At least nothing that will hold up in court."

Sarah shrugged slightly, her expression mirroring my own resignation. "Perhaps you're right," she said, the mood deflating once again. The case was like a maze, and with each turn, we seemed to be facing more walls than exits. Despite the brief moment of camaraderie, the weight of the unsolved case hung heavily between us, a reminder that we were far from finding the answers we desperately needed.

4338.214

(2 August 2018)

THE CONFRONTATION

4338.214.1

Detective Lahey rubbed her hand along my inner thigh, pausing just before it reached my pride. The sensation of her perfectly rounded fingernails riding trails along my thigh sent tingles shooting in all directions. After another heated argument at my house last night, we found a way to make peace that satisfied both of us.

Sarah's hand inched closer, the tips of her fingers stretching to gently touch my crotch. My hands gripped the side of the seat, feeling my arousal strengthen, as Sarah reached underneath, cupping her hands under my balls, squeezing them gently.

I opened my eyes ever so slightly as I glanced over at Sarah, her tongue tracing the outer edges of her lip, hinting at the pleasure still to come.

Secluded in a quiet spot, away from the prying eyes of the precinct, Sarah and I had parked the unmarked police car, allowing ourselves a momentary escape from the relentless pressure of the investigation. The tension between us, compounded by the weight of the case - Gladys, Luke, the bodies we couldn't find, and the one we had - created an atmosphere thick with unsaid words and hidden truths. Neither of us had been brave enough to confess our own dark secrets from the other night. For my part, the need for distraction was becoming increasingly crucial to maintain my sanity.

The sharp squawk of the police radio shattered the silence, jolting us back to reality. "CITY632," it crackled, violently interrupting the moment. I felt a surge of adrenaline as I recognised our callsign. Turning to Sarah, I said with a slight stumble in my voice, "We'd better grab that."

"CITY632, go ahead," Sarah responded, her voice steady and professional.

"CITY632, a disturbance has been reported at a property in Granton. A woman is claiming that a Mr. Luke Smith is on the premises. We've been advised to notify you of any jobs that come up with the name Luke Smith," the dispatch informed us.

"Fuck me!" The words escaped my lips before I could censor them, my hand reflexively pushing Sarah's away from my leg as I started the car's engine. This could be the break we were desperately looking for. "This is it. Tell them we've got it," I ordered, my mind already racing ahead to the possibilities this call presented.

The car's engine roared to life after several revs, the red and blue lights flashing, as I pressed the accelerator, speeding down the street. Sarah quickly coordinated with dispatch over the radio, her fingers deftly jotting down the job details. My heart pounded in my chest, a mix of apprehension and excitement coursing through me. This could be a pivotal moment in the investigation, a chance to finally make some headway in the convoluted web of events that had ensnared us. As the car sped towards Granton, every nerve in my body was alert, my mind acutely focused on the confrontation ahead.

❖

"CITY632, approaching the Jeffries property now," Sarah relayed into the radio, her voice tinged with a barely restrained excitement that mirrored my own heightened state of alertness.

"Copy that CITY632. Proceed with extreme caution. Backup is on its way," the dispatcher responded, their words adding an extra layer of gravity to the situation.

I manoeuvred the car up the rocky, dirt road that snaked its way up the hillside. Each turn seemed to amplify the tension in the car, a tangible sense of anticipation hanging in the air. As a detective, my training had prepared me for confronting the darker aspects of humanity, yet the unpredictability of the job always left room for the unexpected, for those moments that could catch even the most seasoned officer off guard. I was acutely aware of the lines I had crossed in pursuit of Luke, the moral boundaries I had blurred in the name of justice. Today's operation, I firmly reminded myself, would be different. It would be conducted with absolute adherence to protocol.

Jeffries Manor loomed into view, its beautiful sandstone structure standing as a testament to both history and modernity. The new extensions at the front and back of the house lent it an air of elegance and a renewed sense of grandeur. As we pulled to a stop under the shade of a large gum tree, the contrast between the serene beauty of the estate and the potential chaos of our mission was stark.

Sarah, ever ready to spring into action, unbuckled her seatbelt and quickly exited the car, her hand instinctively moving to her gun.

"No gun. Not yet," I cautioned her, my voice firm. I too climbed out of the unmarked car, feeling the crunch of gravel underfoot. The decision to forgo weapons, at least initially, was a deliberate one. In situations like this, the presence of a gun could escalate tensions, and I was determined to approach this with a level of restraint and caution, to ensure we navigated this potentially volatile situation as safely as possible.

As I surveyed Jeffries Manor, my eyes eagerly scanned the scene before us, preparing for any eventuality. The tension was palpable, a mixture of anticipation and readiness that came with years of experience in law enforcement. I held up a hand to Sarah, signalling her to follow my lead. We moved towards the house with cautious, measured steps, our senses heightened, ready to react to any sudden movement or sound.

Before we could even reach the front door to knock, an older woman's voice called out, piercing the stillness of the afternoon. "He's in here," she shouted, her tone laced with urgency and fear.

Instantly, we pivoted towards the source of the voice, our attention drawn to the shed where Louise stood. My heart skipped a beat as I saw her, a figure of desperation and panic, clutching a hefty kitchen knife in her trembling hands. The sight of her, armed and clearly distraught, added an unforeseen layer of complexity to the situation.

"Want to use those guns yet?" Sarah quipped, her question underscored with a hint of dark humour. I could sense the adrenaline coursing through her, the instinctive readiness for action that characterised her as a detective.

Despite the gravity of the situation, I couldn't help but appreciate Sarah's wry sense of humour, a brief moment of levity in an otherwise tense situation. I gave her a quick glance, a silent acknowledgement of her comment, before refocusing on the task at hand.

"We need to deescalate this," I said quietly to Sarah, my mind racing through the best approach to handle Louise without provoking further distress or danger. My training kicked in, reminding me that every action, every word we uttered in these next few moments, could mean the difference between a peaceful resolution and a dangerous escalation.

We cautiously advanced towards the shed, each step measured and deliberate, maintaining a visible distance from our weapons. It was crucial to project an air of non-threatening authority. My voice, steady and reassuring, was ready to address Louise, to convey that we were there to assist and defuse the situation, not escalate it. This was a tightrope walk of policing – asserting control while showing genuine concern.

"Louise Jeffries," I called out to her, my tone firm yet empathetic. "It's time to hand the knife over," I instructed, gesturing towards Sarah, indicating she was to receive the weapon.

Louise, a mix of pride and fear in her eyes, stood waving the knife somewhat erratically. "I've got the bastard trapped inside," she declared, clearly believing she had the upper hand on the situation.

Yet, it was evident she was terrified. Her hands, though gripping the knife, trembled uncontrollably. Sarah, with her usual calm and collected demeanour, coaxed Louise into relinquishing the knife. As she did, the bravado that had momentarily buoyed Louise seemed to evaporate, and she crumbled under the weight of her fear.

"I can't find Brianne!" she sobbed, her voice shaking as she handed over the knife to Sarah. The name didn't immediately register with me.

"Brianne?" I asked, needing clarification.

"Kain's fiancé," Louise explained, her voice tinged with anger and desperation. "Luke came here to talk to her, and now she's gone too," she added, her words fuelling my concern.

"Take her back inside the house," I instructed Sarah firmly. If Louise's claim was true, and Luke was indeed inside the shed, we couldn't afford any distractions. The potential of having an emotionally charged civilian like Louise in the vicinity could complicate matters significantly.

As Sarah escorted Louise back to the safety of the house, I refocused my attention on the shed. The thought that Luke, the elusive and pivotal figure in our investigation, might be mere feet away filled me with a mix of trepidation and determination. This was a moment I had mentally prepared for, but the reality of it was more intense than any rehearsal. My senses were hyper-alert, every nerve primed for the confrontation that was about to unfold. The importance of this encounter was not lost on me; the stakes were extraordinarily high, and the necessity for precise, controlled action was paramount.

Once I saw Sarah and Louise safely enter the house, I turned my full attention to the shed. It was a large structure, its green corrugated iron exterior giving it a robust, albeit somewhat imposing appearance. My hand moved subtly, releasing the clasp of my firearm's holster. While I had no intention of drawing my weapon unless absolutely necessary, readiness was crucial.

"I'm unarmed," a young man's voice announced from within the depths of the shed. My heart rate spiked, adrenaline surging through my body. This had to be Luke. Despite the relatively short duration of our pursuit, it felt as though I had come to know this man deeply, albeit in the most twisted of ways.

With utmost caution, I stepped inside the darkened interior of the shed. The lack of light created a veil of uncertainty, but I was prepared. My gun remained holstered as I raised my hands to visibly show I was not armed. "I just want us to talk," I declared, my voice steady despite the adrenaline coursing through me. I took a few tentative steps forward, my eyes straining to adjust to the dimness, searching for Luke's form in the shadows.

In my mind, I was clear about one thing - if it came down to it, if Luke posed an imminent threat, I wouldn't hesitate to take decisive action, even if that meant shooting him. But for now, my hope was to resolve this situation with words, not bullets. The air was thick with tension, each of my steps measured and cautious, as I moved deeper into the shed.

"I'm Detective Jenkins," I declared, my voice steady despite the adrenaline pumping through me. I was determined to adhere to protocol, to handle this interaction with professionalism. "You must be Luke Smith?" I asked, needing to confirm the identity of the man before me.

"Yes. I am," came the prompt reply from the shadows of the shed.

I pressed on, getting straight to the point. "Where is Brianne?" I questioned, needing to ascertain the whereabouts of Kain's fiancée.

"With Kain," Luke answered, his tone a mix of defensiveness and resignation.

"And where might that be?" I probed further, trying to piece together the scattered fragments of the puzzle, hoping beyond hope that it wasn't a reference to more sinister actions.

"I am not exactly sure. Kain sent her a text message about an hour ago with an address of where to meet him. That's why she took off in his car earlier when I arrived," Luke explained, his voice oddly confident.

I mulled over his response, my mind racing through the implications. "So why is Louise so concerned about her safety?" I asked, trying to understand the reason behind Louise's obvious distress and agitation.

"I don't know. I guess she is just confused and scared. I suppose I would be too if people around me were going missing and being secretive," Luke responded, his words seemingly genuine.

His answer resonated with me; the uncertainty and fear were something I could understand. However, I couldn't shake off the feeling that there was more to this story, layers of complexity and hidden truths that were yet to be uncovered. My instincts as a detective told me that every piece of information, every word spoken, could be a vital clue in unraveling the mystery surrounding the disappearances and Luke's involvement. I knew I had to tread carefully, to parse through his words for any sign of deceit or hidden meaning, while also maintaining a calm and authoritative demeanour. This was a delicate dance, one where a single misstep could have significant consequences.

"Are you being secretive?" I pressed, narrowing my eyes as I studied Luke's demeanour closely.

"No. I really don't know what's going on," he replied, his voice steady, but there was something in his tone, a nuance, that didn't sit right with me.

I fixed Luke with a long, unyielding stare, the dim light of the shed casting shadows that seemed to add to the gravity of our conversation. The air was thick with unspoken accusations and suspicions. "And what about Jamie?" I probed further, feeling a surge of anger welling up within me. My jaw clenched involuntarily as I fought to keep my emotions in check, to maintain the professional detachment necessary in such situations.

"Jamie's safe," Luke answered promptly, his response too quick, too rehearsed.

I didn't believe him. Every instinct in me screamed that he was lying. Luke was a fucking psychopath. After everything that had happened - the disappearances, the deaths - his calmness in the face of such imminent danger was unnerving. Yet, despite my mounting distrust and frustration, my curiosity drove me to ask one more question. "I do have one question for you," I said, breaking the tense silence that had fallen between us.

"What's that?" Luke asked, his shoulders lifting in a nonchalant shrug.

"We tracked your movements to Adelaide just yesterday. How did you manage to sneak past all of our surveillance and back into Hobart?" The question was pivotal; his answer could provide a key insight into his methods and motivations.

Again, Luke simply shrugged, offering no words in response, his silence serving only to fuel my suspicions further.

"You are a cunning little bastard, aren't you," I remarked, a statement rather than a question, as I tried to piece together his elusive game.

The split second Luke's hand moved towards his back pocket, my training kicked in. "Don't move!" I barked, the command erupting from deep within as my hand shot to the holster of my gun. My heart thundered against my ribs, a rapid drumbeat of adrenaline and instinct. In these critical moments, the line between order and chaos was vanishingly thin, my heightened senses razor-focused on the unfolding threat.

Luke's sudden movement was abrupt, a motorbike in the shed clattering to the floor with a resounding crash. I didn't give myself time to think; I reacted on pure instinct. With all the force I could muster, I charged at Luke, my shoulder leading. The impact was solid, striking him squarely in the chest. I felt the satisfying yet jarring sensation of the hit as Luke's breath whooshed out, his body reeling from the blow. We both tumbled to the floor in a tangle of limbs.

Scrambling to gain the upper hand, I moved quickly, my training guiding every motion. Sitting up on my knees, I manoeuvred my body over Luke's. With my left leg, I positioned myself strategically, securing his right arm in a textbook wrist lock. Luke's reaction was immediate – a sharp jerk of pain. He rolled, instinctively trying to escape, his movement catching my leg.

I struggled briefly to maintain control, a few beads of sweat breaking out on my forehead from the intensity of the altercation. With Luke now on his back, I pinned his arms above his head on the cold concrete floor, squatting firmly on his waist to immobilise him.

In the aftermath of the scuffle, I found myself in an unusual position. Conventionally, a suspect would be lying face down, but here we were, Luke on his back and me looming over him, our hands locked in a stalemate. We stared at each other, the tension thick in the air. I was momentarily unsure of my next move. This wasn't a conventional arrest; it was raw and unscripted. My mind raced for the next step, but in that brief, charged moment, time seemed to stand still. The urgency of the situation was palpable, yet I was acutely aware of the need to handle this delicately. Every decision now could have lasting repercussions.

"Well, this is awkward," Luke finally broke the tense silence, his voice almost casual.

I shot him a perplexed look, baffled by his nonchalance. *How could he not be terrified in this situation?* "You're enjoying this, aren't you?" I accused, disgust tainting my words. I couldn't fathom how he could remain so composed under these circumstances.

Luke met my intense gaze without flinching. "And what about you?" he retorted, a grin creeping across his face as if he found some twisted amusement in our standoff.

"If my hands weren't pinning you down right now, I'd punch you in the face," I snapped back, my patience wearing thin. Protocol was the last thing on my mind at this point. A part of me, the part fuelled by anger and frustration, fantasised about ending this once and for all, imagining my hands free to act on the rage simmering within me.

"Well, ain't that a shame," Luke replied with a wink, adding fuel to the fire of my growing fury.

"You're a fucking psychopath," I hissed at him, the words barely audible as I struggled to keep my anger in check.

"What makes you think I'm a psychopath?" Luke challenged, his tone almost mocking.

"Do you have no remorse for what you've done?" I demanded, my voice rising with each word. "You've murdered at least four people!"

"I haven't murdered anyone!" Luke shot back defensively, his eyes widening in what seemed like genuine surprise. "Have you?" he suddenly asked, his expression turning to one of fear.

His question hit me like a physical blow, sending a chill down my spine. The memories of the past few days, the haunting images and actions, flashed through my mind in a rapid, disorienting succession. Doubt crept into my thoughts. *What if I'm wrong? What if Luke is actually innocent?* The possibility, however remote, gnawed at me. Against my better judgment, I eased my grip on Luke's arms slightly, the tension in my shoulder becoming increasingly uncomfortable.

As I adjusted my position, a myriad of emotions and thoughts collided within me. The line between right and wrong, guilt and innocence, seemed to blur, leaving me in a state of uncertainty and confusion. The situation was far from black and white, and I found myself grappling with the complexities of the case, the decisions I had made, and the actions I was prepared to take. The moment was pivotal, a turning point that could redefine everything I thought I knew about the investigation and about myself.

"So, how do you want to do this?" I asked, a pragmatic edge to my voice. I was eager to stand up, to move away from this physical stalemate. As I waited for Luke's response, a sudden, unsettling sensation washed over me. The fine hairs on the back of my neck stood on end, a primitive alarm system responding to an unseen threat. My radio crackled loudly, breaking the tense silence, adding to the sudden surge of apprehension.

Above us, the lone light near the shed's entrance flickered ominously, casting erratic shadows across the interior. My eyes widened, my mind momentarily hijacked by haunting memories - the sinister sight of a room filled with black garbage bags and that chilling, disembodied voice whispering, "Bye, Karl." A shiver coursed down my spine, a physical manifestation of the dread these memories evoked.

My introspection was abruptly shattered by a young, female voice from behind, catching me completely off guard. "Beatrix?" I whispered, my confusion palpable. Gently, I shifted my weight off Luke's waist, just enough to turn my head and see who had called out. The name echoed in my mind, a tether to a different part of this complex puzzle.

But the moment I turned, I realised my error. I winced in agony as Luke's knee connected forcefully with my groin. The sharp, debilitating pain was immediate, overwhelming any other response. Instinctively, my hands left their hold on Luke, moving to clutch at the source of my pain.

As the searing pain from Luke's knee strike coursed through me, I anticipated his next move would be to escape. But to my utter astonishment, instead of wriggling free, Luke threw himself forward. In a split second, I was thrown backward, our bodies locked in a chaotic tangle.

As we grappled in the dim light of the shed, the darkness around us seemed to dissolve into an array of brilliant, swirling colours, as if reality itself was shifting. The scene was surreal, almost hallucinogenic. "Welcome to Clivilius, Karl Jenkins," a voice echoed in my mind, a silent, eerie whisper that seemed to resonate from the very depths of my consciousness.

The clamour of the shed's contents crashing around us faded into a distant, muffled hum, overshadowed by the intensity of the moment. The throbbing pain in my groin, though still acute, became a secondary concern as I wrestled with Luke, our bodies rolling through the dust and debris.

We struggled fiercely, each of us fighting for dominance in this bizarre and unexpected confrontation. Finally, I managed to manoeuvre Luke onto his back, pinning his hands above his head. The situation felt eerily familiar, a strange sense of déjà vu washing over me. *Not again*, I thought to myself, my mind reeling.

As the bizarre and unsettling distortions faded away, I found myself firmly anchored back in the grim reality of the situation. The surreal experience, though fleeting, had left me disoriented and doubting my own senses. What had felt almost dreamlike was now replaced by the unyielding truth of the moment - Luke Smith pinned beneath me, and the cold, hard concrete of the Jeffries' shed floor beneath us both. The gravity of what had just transpired hit me with full force.

My head spun as I tried to regain my bearings, my eyes focusing on the immediate clutter of the shed that blurred with the various shades of brown dust, contrasting starkly against the backdrop of a cloudless blue sky. The anger I felt toward Luke, which had briefly subsided in the confusion of the moment, began to resurface, boiling over as I saw him lying in the dust, grinning provocatively at me. "Bye, Karl," he whispered, his voice a sinister echo in my ears.

In a fit of rage, driven by the tumultuous emotions and the chaos of the situation, I delivered a hard punch to Luke's head. The impact of my fist against his skull was sharp and decisive, enough to render him unconscious. "Fuck you!" I shouted at his now motionless body, releasing some of the pent-up frustration and fury.

Suddenly, a sea of voices approached, breaking the isolation of our struggle. I quickly rolled off Luke and scrambled to my feet, acutely aware of the approaching crowd. In a reflexive motion, I grabbed my gun, squinting as my eyes adjusted to the harsh sunlight.

"Stay back!" I commanded, waving the gun with a shaky hand at the approaching figures. "I'll shoot," I warned, my voice carrying an edge of desperation. The situation was rapidly spiralling out of my control. The adrenaline, fear, and confusion mingled, creating a volatile mix that threatened to overwhelm my usually composed demeanour.

As the figures drew closer, I realised the gravity of what I was doing - brandishing a weapon at fellow officers and bystanders. My training and instincts screamed at me to de-escalate, to regain control not only of the situation but of myself. But the aftermath of the surreal encounter with Luke, coupled with the intense emotions it had stirred up, left me teetering on the brink of losing my grasp on the situation.

"Karl!" The sound of a woman's voice cut through the tense air, momentarily drawing my attention away from the chaos. I hadn't noticed her initially, but there she was – Beatrix, her long, silver hair framing her face, creating an almost ethereal presence amidst the turmoil.

For a fleeting moment, I considered lowering my weapon, her familiar presence almost calming. But I couldn't. The confusion and fear were too overwhelming.

"What the fuck is Clivilius?" I demanded, my voice laced with desperation and confusion, the words almost a spray of saliva. My gun remained unflinchingly aimed at Beatrix's chest.

"This place," Beatrix replied with an eerie calmness, her hands gesturing broadly as if to encompass our surroundings. "Karl," she continued, her voice soft and soothing, "It's okay."

Another gaze caught my attention, pulling my focus away from Beatrix. Squinting, I tried to discern the face in the crowd. "Jamie?" I whispered, barely audible, a mix of confusion and disbelief in my voice.

My breaths became deeper, more laboured, as I struggled to make sense of the scene unfolding before me. Suddenly, the gun in my hand felt like a foreign object, and it dropped from my grasp, hitting the dust with a soft thud.

As my head spun, a wave of nausea overwhelmed me. I barely registered the young, tall man stepping forward from the group, his hand extended in a gesture of introduction. "Hi, I'm Paul Smith," he said cheerfully, an incongruous note in the otherwise tense atmosphere. "Luke's brother," he added, glancing briefly at Luke, who now seemed to stir with a strange vitality.

A surge of blood rushed to my head, a wave of warmth flooding my body. I blinked rapidly, trying to dispel the fuzziness clouding my mind. "Shit!" I cried out, a terror gripping me. "I'm dead!"

The world around me began to fade, my mind succumbing to the darkness that loomed on the edges of my consciousness. My body, no longer able to support itself, collapsed into the dust, surrendering to the overwhelming sensations and the inexplicable events that had just transpired. The last thing I remember was the ground rushing up to meet me, and then nothing but darkness.

TO BE CONTINUED...

Printed and bound by CPI Group (UK) Ltd, Croydon, CR0 4YY
21/07/2024
01020035-0005